For Geoffery Madsen
from his uncle

John Weld

Christmas 1981

THE MISSIONARY

A novel of the
early SouthWest

by John Weld

NORTHWOODS PRESS   Stafford, Va.

ISBN 0-89002-175-9, paper
ISBN 0-89002-176-7, cloth

Library of Congress Catalog Card Number:

AMERICAN HISTORY PRESS
Division of:
NORTHWOODS PRESS
PO Box 249
Stafford, VA 22554 USA

Sometimes I think that the power of a priest is in proportion to the ignorance and superstition of the people he serves, that he must convince them to believe as true what reason tells them is false.

From the private journal of Father Georgio Moreno.

CHAPTER ONE

Two gray-frocked Franciscan frairs knelt side by side in the little adobe chapel which had been named for Saint James. They were imploring God to preserve the good ship *Santa Maria* which had been despatched to bring supplies to this little-known harbor in Alta, California. The shorter, stouter of the priests was intense, impassioned, hypnotic Junipero Serra, he of the game leg. His pleas were fervent. The life of his ambitious enterprise—to found a chain of Missions along the California coast—was dependent upon the umbilical cord which the sihp represented. Without its nourishment the endeavor would surely die.

Having already established the Missions San Diego, San Carlos, San Gabriel, San Antonio and San Luis Obispo, Father Serra had requisitioned the apostolic College of San Fernando, in the city of Mexico, for two priests with whom to found another at a place two days' journey to the north of San Diego. Presumably they and the necessary food, seed, animals and accouterments were aboard the overdue ship.

"To harvest souls for your Heavenly garden," Father Serra was saying, "we need worldly goods—beads for one thing, and a bell. Without beads we cannot so readily gain the good will and confidence of the natives, and without a bell to toll Your Almighty Voice, oh Father, a chapel lacks a soul. Besides which," the good Father President of the California Missions went on, shifting his weight a little to favor his lame leg, "it is highly necessary that we have cloth to clothe the natives' nakedness and, of course, cattle and sheep for tallow and meat. Without tallow one cannot have candles; and what, Dear Father, is Mass without candles? And then there are images of Jesus and the Virgin Mary and the vestments and the vessels of silver. One cannot found a Mission without these things which are aboard the *Santa Maria*. Hasten her hither, I pray Thee. Let her not suffer the fate of the *San Jose*"—The Father President was recalling to God's sometimes forgetful mind a ship, sent out with the first expedition,

5

which, after rounding Cape San Lucas, vanished forever.

The other supplicant was a large man with a bulbous nose, thick black eyebrows over deep-set, soft, brown eyes, and a big mouth clamped into firmness by a cleft, stubbled chin. He had recently come to San Diego from the Mission Santa Gertrudis in Baja California, a sandal's life to the south. There he had spent a year administering to the parched natives and saving their souls. Thereto he had spent eleven years in the Sierra Gordo, on the mainland of Mexico, doing likewise. His interest in the *Santa Maria* was more personal. She was to take him to Mexico City where he was to teach at the College of San Fernando. Thus his prayers were no less fervent than Father Serra's. Weary of isolation and loneliness, he yearned to return to the intellectual stimulation of civilization.

"When I was younger," he explained to God, not uttering the words, merely speaking them in his mind, and saying almost word for word that he had told Father Serra, "I was excited by the prospect of working among savages, bringing them Your Word and drawing them into the Church, and it has been a rewarding experience. But I find now that my interest lags. I ask your forgiveness for my selfishness, but I long to work in a more cultural climate, to save the truly sinful rather than convert the ignorant. . ."

Disturbingly from outside came utterances of profanity, and Father Moreno excused himself to God, made the sign of the cross, arose, genuflected and retreated from the altar. He passed from the shadowed, cool interior of the adobe chapel into the stark brilliance of midday sunshine and spoke sharply to the boy: "Pepito!—"

The boy, quarrelling with a man over a burro, turned to look at the priest. He was tall for his twelve years, very slender and with a spiritual face reminiscent, save that it was dark skinned, of the child Jesus. "Yes, Father?" Velvet black eyes looked innocently at the cleric. Long since Pepito had learned to put forth a front of virtue and reverence to hide his roughish nature.

"What mischief are you up to now?" Father Moreno advanced on much-worn, patched sandals. His gray garment was somewhat short for his big frame, it having shrunk from many washings. The fringe of black hair on his tonsured head grew down over the tops of his ears.

"It is not me," the boy said, looking as if guilt were a stranger, "is Vincenti," indicating the fat man who wore the leather vest and helmet of a soldier. "He hit me."

"You, Vincenti—you should be ashamed of yourself!" And the

6

priest silently admonished himself: *I have no judgement where Pepito is concerned.* The boy, a native Californian, was like a son to him. He had "adopted" him at Santa Gertrudis.

"He tried to lick me here," the soldier said, rubbing his groin.

"Then you must have provoked him," Father Moreno said.

"He want to kill Mirable, Father," the boy said, indicating the burro. "He want to eat her."

"We are hungry, Father," Vincenti said.

"We are all hungry," Father Moreno said. "But we cannot kill our beasts of burden." He rubbed Mirabel's nose and she tried to bite his hand. "She, too, is hungry," he observed wryly. "If the ship does not come we will have to move south. Who will carry the water?"

"Yes," Pepito said, emboldened by the defense, "who will carry the water?"

"Not Vincenti," the priest said. "He is too fat. Now you two behave yourselves." About to reenter the chapel, Father Moreno paused, his attention arrested, and gazed, squinting fixedly at something in the distance. *Could it be?* Away out on the heat-scrimmed horizon was something that looked like a sail! The priest closed his eyes and looked again. It was still there, as sure as Heaven. *Glory be to God and to the Son and to the Holy Ghost!* "A sail! A sail!" he shouted from the doorway to Father Serra.

It required almost three hours for the ship to reach the shallows and drop anchor. Eventually two small boats were lowered. The first brought the captain, the second a priest; and, even as the first set out, sailors aboard the ship began pushing cattle into the bay so that they could swim to shore.

Father Moreno, his skirts tucked into his waistcord, went into the water to help land the captain's skiff as it came sliding down a swell onto the sand. After exchanging embraces the captain told the priest that strong winds had blown them off course. They had beaten their way back only to be becalmed for nine days. Meanwhile Father Serra was welcoming the newly arrived cleric, a slender young man whose most notable feature were his pale blue eyes. The latter had brought a letter from the Father Guardian of the College of San Fernando:

Dear Father Serra:

This will serve to introduce Father Salvatore Trujillo whom we are sending to assist you in your vast vineyard.

7

You requested two brothers for the new Mission, but the bearer of this letter is the only one we can for the present spare.

The Father President looked appraisingly at the frail newcomer, confirming his first impression.

Father Trujillo said, "They are very short handed at the College," apologetically.

The Father President returned to the letter:

We send him to you with our prayers. He is very determined to harvest souls, and in this respect I think he is almost as zealous as thyself, if this be possible. In any case, we entrust him to your great heart. . .

"Did you bring any skills?" the Father President asked the young priest. "I mean, do you have any knowledge of building? Are you a stone-mason, perhaps? Do you know how to make mud bricks?"

Father Trujillo's eyelids fluttered. "I have been trained as an architect," he said.

"Ah, an architect!—Why, that's wonderful."

"The Father Guardian thought I might be useful."

"Indeed you will be. At the new Mission you will erect a fine cathedral to the glory of God."

"That is my aspiration."

Father Serra put an arm about the younger priest's shoulders. "And I will help you in every way I can."

Later in Father Moreno's adobe cell, Father Serra handed his fellow priest the letter from the Father Guardian. Father Moreno read it, handed the letter back to his superior and looked directly into his eyes. "I see the situation hasn't changed."

Father Serra said, "I cannot send him up there alone. He is too young and inexperienced."

Father Moreno sighed resignedly.

"I hate to ask you to stay, Georgio, but I really have no choice. You can teach him so much.

"You flatter me."

"You will be doing me—and God—a great favor."

8

"I am happy to go where I am needed."

"God will reward you."

The two men embraced. Without further word, the Father President went outside and Father Moreno sat down, obviously dejected. Indeed, his disappointment was so strong that he felt guilty. He closed his eyes and spoke to God as in confession: "Oh, Father, please forgive me for my despair. I had hoped that I could serve you better in the byways of civilization than here in this barren wilderness. But I realize that there is much of Your work to be done here among the wild infidels, and of course, as Your servant, I will perform as you direct me. As a priest I must sublimate my personal desires and do only that which pleases You. I shall swallow my sorrow and do all that I can to bring the savages into the fold."

He then got a piece of his precious paper from his journal and wrote to his sister:

My Dear Josefina:

The ship which brings this letter to you was to have removed me from this distant outpost to Mexico, whence I hoped eventually to come home to Spain; but due to the shortage of missionaries Father Serra has asked me to remain and help found a new Mission at a place two days' journey hence. Of course I shall do so. I am happy to serve God in any way and in may place He dictates. A young priest, Father Salvatore Trujillo, from Cadiz, arrived today and he and I will work together to found the Mission and convert the heathen. My heart goes out to him, for I well know what frustrations and hardships lie ahead. He has left the comforts and protection of civilization to endure this very difficult life in a wilderness among a wild and pagan people, a people without religion or laws, honor or shame. They occupy themselves with nothing but their bodily appetites, which they have in common with animals. It will be our task to bring to them the word of God and to educate them in morality, hygiene and justice. No mean task. I will celebrate my forty-ninth birthday next month. I am in good health. I trust this find you well. I pray for you every day. May God bless you. Your brother in Christ,

Georgio

He had written to his sister the year before, from Santa Gertrudis, telling her that, after almost ten years in California he had asked to be returned to the College of San Fernando in Mexico City.

I fervently want to return to civilization, he wrote, *and I need to tell you why. What I am going to say I would utter to no one else, and I tell you because I trust you and because I must tell someone to quiet my tormented mind.*

I am disillusioned. When I entered the priesthood I was youthfully idealistic. The Church was the sacred world and the priesthood was its highest order. In the thirty years I have done its bidding, mostly in the wilderness among savages, I have learned a great deal. I have learned that the Church is complicated and that it is powerful. It prides itself on being the one true religion in the world, and my trouble is that I have begun to wonder about that. I wonder if we are not deluding ourselves. Maybe other religions are good too. The Catholic Church is a gigantic body and we who work in it are endeavoring to enlarge it by proselytizing. We call it saving souls. Well, I wonder if that is what we are doing here among the Indians of far-off California. The poor natives I have "converted" are as lazy and good-for-nothing as ever. They had their own barbaric religion before I came and it probably served them as well as what I am teaching.

You can imagine that this kind of heretic thinking has distressed me. I am tortured. The pain is excruciating. I have tried to blank such thoughts from my mind because I have been taught that they are evil. But they keep coming back. I am beginning to believe that they are not evil and that I am wasting my time here, my life. That is why I want to return to work among those of my own kind.

Let me hasten to reassure you that I have not lost my faith in God or my belief in the Bible. And I cling tenaciously to the Catholic Church because it is my haven in this turbulent world.

Now there. I have said what I desperately needed to say. I hope, my dear sister, you won't condemn me.

Your brother in Christ,

Georgio

The short, thick Commandant of the small garrison at San Diego, Lieutenant Ortega, lined up four soldiers for the priest's inspection. They were a motley lot. Besides the fat Vincenti Escudero, there was Pedro Vargas, who had a hare lip, prodruding ears and, although quite young, receding hair. Next was Falco Santiago, a dark villainous-looking fellow with tightly curled jet-black hair and a moustache which turned down at both ends. The fourth was Jose Cabenza whose clothing was too ample for his spare frame. All were stubble-bearded and as they lined up before Fathers Moreno and Trujillo they looked less like soldiers of the Spanish King than derelicts.

"There's one more," the Commandant said. "Their sergeant. He's in jail."

"What for?"

"Rape, Father."

"Since when did they start putting soldiers in jail for that?" Father Trujillo asked.

Father Moreno said, "It may not be rape in the legal sense. Indeed, in all probability the lady cooperated. But we have a strict rule that soldiers may not cohabit with native women unless they marry them. We priests cannot preach the word of God on the one hand while on the other the soldiers break the commandments. To win and hold these pagan people's confidence we and they must practice what we preach. The success or failure of the new Mission will depend on our behavior."

Vincenti said: "They promised us they were going to send women from Mexico."

"Promises, promises," Falco said.

"They've forgotten us," Vincenti said.

The Commandant led the way to the *calabozo* and unbolted the door. "Hey, Ignacio—"

The prisoner was lying on a bull-hide bunk. He raised his head, his eyes blinking against the sudden sunlight. He was a man in his late twenties whose clothes, though much the worse for wear, fit him with some fidelity. Tall and slender with the lean hip and thigh of a bullfighter, he got up and came to the doorway, stood leaning against the jamb. His dirty hair was a light brown, his eyes were speckled with gold, and there was a certain indefinable air of quality and independence about him.

The Commandant addressed him: "You're going with the padres to found a new mission."

"Afternoon, Father," Ignacio said, speaking to Father Moreno, eyes puckered against the strong sunshine. "I hear you're going to leave us."

"No, Ignacio, I am going to stay here and try and save your soul," Father Moreno said wryly.

Ignacio grinned. "I don't know why you're so concerned about it. Such as it is, it doesn't bother me."

"If we permit you to come with us," the priest said, "I want you to promise me you'll let the women alone."

"I'm no priest. I didn't take any vows of chastity, Father."

"I'm asking you to take one now."

"I'll do the best I can, but you might as well ask a man to go without eating."

The Commandant said, "If he gives you any trouble, Father, let me know."

Ignacio smiled unconcernedly.

Father Moreno said, "We leave tomorrow."

"I'm ready," the soldier said.

CHAPTER TWO

Round, voluptuous hills lay sleeping against the pale, heat-scrimmed sky as the caravan of men and livestock moved slowly Northward, plodding the dusty flatland between the lomas and the sea. The afternoon sun sucked thirstily at parched grass and prickly pear, at volcanic rock and lizard, and its infinite rays struck a myriad of scintillations from the vast and tranquil Pacific. Buzzards circled lazily, warily, not moving a black feather, obsidian eyes peeled in death watch, nostrils tuned for stench. Nowhere was there a tree or a roof to relieve the stark brilliance, and the only solace from the heat was a soft zephyr which swept eastward as the world whirled.

At the head of the straggly procession, *cuera* across his knees, a hand on his upright lance, his leather helmet cocked almost comically to shield his face from the declining sun, rod Ignacio, soldier in the army of His Majesty King Carlos III and escort of the Roman Catholic Church. Behind him trudged Fathers Serra and Moreno, the latter leading the burro Mirable. Pepito followed shepherding eight burros, four horses, nine cows, two heifers, four calves, a bull and four sheep. The burros, save for Mirable, were loaded with various burdens, including crates of chickens; they carried bobbing heads tired-low. Bringing up the rear were the other soldiers, the fat Vincenti, Pedro the harelip, the dark, almost black Falco and the half-asleep José.

Ignacio leaned relaxedly on the pommel of his saddle watching his horse's ears flop springlessly and pondering the reasons which had brought him to this dehydrated, God-forsaken place. There was the land he and the other volunteers had been promised once they had completed their enlistments; but owning land here, he thought, would be like owning the sky. There was enough of it, he reckoned, for everyone in the world to have as much as he could see. Father Moreno's voice interrupted his reverie.

"Let us wait a little," the priest said. "Wait for the water mule. Can you see Father Trujillo?"

The soldier lifted his thin haunches from the sweaty saddle to look back. "No Father." For two days the young priest had been suffering from what the soldiers called Montezuma's revenge and it was some time before he came trudging along, his jaws taut.

"Are you all right?" the Father President asked.

Father Trujillo managed a grim smile. "The Lord is testing me," he said.

Father Serra said, "We are almost there—another two hours."

"Alas we have no blackberry cordial," Father Moreno said. "It is a good remedy for diarrhea. My mother used to give it to me when I was a child. Fool that I was, I used to dislike it. I classed it with other medicines such as castor oil and sulphur. It was not until I grew up that I learned its virtues."

The ailing priest gave no indication that he had heard.

Father Serra said, "Father Moreno and I have been discussing a name for the new Mission. Today is October twenty-eighth, San Simeon's day. We thought to name the new Mission for Him. How does that strike you, Father?"

"A happy choice." the young priest said. "The Lord has led us to this place this day and He Himself has named it."

"I expect you and Father Moreno to have the finest Mission of all," the Father President went on. "The important thing, remember, is to baptize." And, launched on his favorite topic, Father Serra became passionate and intense. The fanaticism which was always close to the surface in him emerged. "Baptize and baptize some more. Baptize them and they will stay with you. We must appeal to the heathen in every way we know, through pageantry and music and symbol and sign, through pomp and ceremony, the laying on of hands and the unction of the sick. If love doesn't work, persuade and if persuasion doesn't work, coerce. God has sent us to save these poor pagans and we must not fail Him." The Father President then spoke directly to Father Trujillo. "At first it will seem impossible that you can teach the Californians to labor, because they have no experience with nor inclination for it. You will be frustrated; discouragement will eat at your heart. But you must ever keep in mind that you are bringing these poor gentiles the beauty, the security and the enlightenment of the true faith; you are preparing them for the life hereafter, and you are doing it for their sakes and for the glory of God. . ."

At this pause Father Trujillo hastily excused himself and, abruptly lifting his skirt to give his legs more freedom, darted away to the shade of a clump of mesquite.

Father Moreno still had hold of Mirabel's halter, but she was trying to extend her grazing area, so he let her go. He called to Pepito, he of the boney knees and big feet: "Bring me a cow, the one with the most milk."

The boy was quick to comply. "This one, he has got the most," he hollered and, looping a rope about her neck, drew one out of the procession. Her calf came with her.

"It's for Father Trujillo," the padre said.

Pepito's face clouded. "We have no bucket."

Father Moreno asked, "You know what means invention?" unconsciously falling into the lad's speech rhythm. Pepito shook his head. "Is what you use when you have nothing else." The big man smiled and cuffed the boy on the shoulder. "When you have no bucket," he went on, and tapped his temple with a finger, "you use your head, your brain. You think of something. That is invention."

"Si," the boy said, not fully comprehending. And he repeated the word *invention*, trying it awkwardly on his tongue.

When presently Father Trujillo rejoined them, he was persuaded to get on his hands and knees while Father Moreno squeezed milk into his mouth. The cow was submissive enough, but having been driven many miles the past two days her udder was not munificent, and it required a strong pull to draw the milk. This made hitting the target difficult, and the ailing priest's face was soon dripping. Meanwhile the cow's calf stood by eyeing the proceedings with raised ears. After a considerable effort Father Trujillo lay back exhausted, a hand over his eyes to block out the strong light of the sun.

The others moved on, but Father Moreno, after retrieving Mirabel's halter, sat down to keep Father Trujillo company. "Trouble with this country," he said to make conversation, "is that there're no trees—at least none with leaves large enough to aid a man in your distress."

The sick priest gave no indication that he appreciated the humor, and Father Moreno quickly shut off a misgiving. There was no good in bringing doubt to the relationship at the outset. Time was required for them to know each other and to make necessary personality adjustments.

When presently Father Trujillo was able to proceed, Father Moreno urged him to ride a way and offered him Mirabel's halter, but the sick man declined and went on ahead, weaving drunkenly. Father

15

Moreno shrugged eloquently, stepped aside and drew the burro up to him. "In that case," he said quietly, "I ask you and our seraphic father, Saint Francis, to absolve me. I am going to rest my feet for a mile or two." And, as much to shame Father Trujillo as to relieve himself, the stoic proceeded, though not without difficulty, to mount the animal. The skirt of his habit drawn high, his long, hairy legs dangling comically, his big sandaled feet all but dragging ground, he sat urging the incongruously small beast to motion. "*Sic,*" he sucked. "Get ye gone!" But the burro, a little brown lady with dark hairs around eyes and mouth, shook her head as if in reply and did not move a hoof. In her mischievous expression it was evident that Mirabel was more than a beast of burden, that she was wise beyond her ken and years. She knew the man on her back very well; they had served God together in Baja California. "Mirabella," the priest said to her now, speaking more calmly, for experience had taught him that she responded more readily to gentle tones than to bellowing, "do you hear me?—I want you to get thee gone." Still the burro did not budge, and it may have been, as Father Moreno sometimes suspected, she had a seventh sense, for it was just then that her owner, defender and protector, Pepito, came running. "No, no, Father," the boy protested, somewhat out of breath. "You too heavy, Father!"

"It is not that I am heavy," Father Moreno said. "She has carried far more weight than mine. It is simply that she is obstinate beyond measure. She has no respect for the cloth. Truly, I think there is the Devil in her." He slid off the burro's back and rubbed his buttock. "Furthermore, she is as hard as experience."

The boy leapt upon the burro's back and almost in the same motion kicked her with his bare heels. Without hesitation Mirabel trotted off with him finally breaking into an easy, rocking-chair gallop. Pepito looked back, grinning triumphantly.

The priest smiled, feeling less apprehensive about the future, and trudged on. By way of apology he said to God: "I only wanted to ride a little way."

The sun was still two hours above the horizon when the caravan descended to an almost dry riverbed fringed with willows and bulrushes. Here and there along the meager stream a mottled sycamore stretched gnarled arms, and the riverbed itself, made broad by spring floods, was a welter of rounded granite stones.

"Praise be to God!" Father Serra intoned, scooping up a handful of the precious water. "I name thee Rio San Simeon! May the good saint provide you with water for our labors here!"

Father Trujillo dropped to his knees, rosary and missel clasped to his chest. Father Moreno looked about him, at the men and stock drinking, heard the strong but gentle sound of the ocean as it swelled upon the shore, watched a flock of pelicans rise lazily from the estuary and glide away. And suddenly, unaccountably it was all familiar to him, unaccountably because, while the scene was similar in typography to Baja California and to certain parts of southern Spain, he had never to his knowledge passed this way before. And yet the way the hills parted to make the valley, the way the valley fluted to the sea, the way the fringes of tules followed the flood-torn banks, the color of the rocks, the recurrent sound of the waves spewing upon the shore, even the smells were strongly familiar to him. He tried to hang on to the memory that he might examine its source, but he got only a glimpse before it was gone. It was as if the rare insight had glowed in but one cell of him. It was tantalizing because he suspected that in that brief glimpse he had perceived a clue to the mystery that is time.

The little band of men and beasts moved up the rocky riverbed to a grove of live oak trees, far enough from the sea not to be vulnerable to the guns of hostile ships. Here, on a knoll chosen the year before by Father Serra, the Mission would be built.

While soldiers and muleteers unpacked the animals, the padres raised the cross and set about making a bower of branches and red velvet. A table was improvised and covered with white linen, and thereon were placed the altarstone, crucifix, lighted candles in silver sticks, chalice, paten, and ciborium properly arranged for the ceremony of Mass. A banner, crudely painted with almost life-size images of the Virgin Mary and Child Jesus, was hung above the altar. While Father Serra prepared himself for the ceremony, donning alb, chasuble, stole and amice, bells were hung from the limb of an oak, and these when he was ready, the Father President began ringing with great intensity. "Come! Come!—Pagan brothers, come!" he shouted. "Come to the House of the Lord!—Come and receive the Gospel of Christ which we have brought to you!" And aside to his fellow priests he said, "This is a dark hour for ignorance and evil."

Presently there appeared, advancing cautiously through the brush, a group of natives escorted by half a dozen rib-wrapped whelps. The males were naked, but the females wore deerskin aprons before and behind, and several wore rabbit-fur coverings over their breasts. The women without exception wore shell bracelets and necklaces. In toto the Californians were a motley, comic, even ludicrous lot, but the Father President saw them only as souls to be saved. "We have come from far, far away to bring you the word of God," he told them, speaking in Spanish and waiting for Father Moreno and Pepito to translate as best they could. "We are messengers from your Heavenly Father," he then went on, impassioned. "And from the King of Spain. We have come to feed you when you are hungry, and to heal you when you are sick, and to prepare you for the hereafter!"

In the forefront of the group was a short but well proportioned young man in his early twenties. His only adornment was a band of grasses on his head. He listened without expression to the strange words. When a pause occurred he began speaking animatedly, apparently taking it for granted that he should respond and that he would be understood. He rattled on at length, interspersing his remarks with elaborate gestures. At the conclusion of his speech, Pepito translated: "He say they know God, Father. He say God live on roof of mountain. Him call Chinigchinich. Him make lightening and rain."

"No, no, no!" Father Serra exclaimed. "That is not right! Tell him he is confusing God with the Devil. Tell them God is their Father, that He rules the world and the stars, that He is good, that He is wise, that He is just."

The Indians listened solemnly, though it was obvious they understood little. Apparently they were satisfied with their own interpretation of God and believed that these men who dressed from necks to feet came from Chinigchinich. In their diffidence and humility they did what they thought would be pleasing to these heavenly emissaries: they began to dance. While the women and children clapped their hands in an off-beat rhythm, the men proceeded, slowly at first, then faster, to stomp their feet, to twist and turn, to writhe and bend, to gyrate and jump, now squatting now rising, the while giving forth a cacophony of shouts, hoots and wails.

One of the women a breast cupped in a hand, approached the banner depicting the Virgin and Child, a gesture which mightily pleased Father Serra who believed the woman inately recognized the Son of God. "They sense the holiness of the images!" he cried.

In an effort to quiet the natives so that Mass could be celebrated, the Father President ordered beads to be distributed and himself sowed these seeds of civilization. "Tell them we are going to talk with God," he instructed Pepito.

The natives, ecstatic at the prospect of acquiring the brightly colored glass beads, pushed for positions to receive them. As the two priests doled them out, Father Trujillo said to Father Moreno, "I wonder about giving them beads. Should we bribe people to come into the Church?"

"Beads are a means to an end."

"But they appeal to the avarice in these people. Can the end be good if the means of reaching it is evil?"

Father Moreno shrugged. "Hogs eat swill, but roast pork is delicious."

Throughout the Mass the natives stood quietly in awe, but during the spirited but tedius sermon, not a word of which they could understand, they became restless. Again their young spokesman broke in with an harangue, slapping his thighs and shouting words he thought appropriate to the occasion. It was an embarassing situation—the man of God and the heathen expatiating at the same time—so Father Moreno went over to the Californian and tried to make him understand that God would be displeased unless he desisted. The young man must have misunderstood what was expected of him, for he renewed his harangue, speaking even more loudly and excitedly and gesticulating even more wildly. He sounded as if he were rejecting the Spaniards and damning them to Hell, whereas in truth he was welcoming them and making a pledge of friendship. Father Moreno had joined the oratory, raising his voice to outshout the Indian; but the latter ignored the interruption, apparently considering it a part of the ceremony. Seemingly hypnotized by his own rhetoric, he went on shouting and gesticulating. In desperation, Father Moreno took a calculated risk: he seized the young man, flung him to the ground and, by twisting an arm behind his back, held him there until the Father President had concluded his sermon. He then released the Indian, shook his hand, apologized and made over him the sign of the cross.

"Had he overcome me," Father Moreno said later to Father Trujillo, "he and his people would have held us all in contempt."

The young man was awed by the priest's dexterousness and strength; instead of the resentment Father Moreno expected, he evinced an idolatrous respect for him. Using gestures to supplement his Chumash words, the Indian held out his hands to the priest and indicated they were his to use as he would.

Because of his zany personality and because his Chumash name, meaning rain-on-the-mountain was unpronouncable, the young Indian spokesman became known as El Loco. The name suited him well. He was flippant, light-minded, high-spirited and mocking. In conversation it was difficult to tell whether he was serious or joshing. Unpredictably, while conversing, he might break into a dance or perform some acrobatic act such as standing on his hands.

He became the Mission's first convert. Several factors figured in his decision to come live at the Mission. One was his respect for Father Moreno. Another was the bribe of trousers and a shirt, a costume which gave him the distinction he craved.

When Father Moreno gave him the garments, El Loco donned the trousers at once, leaving his genitals hanging out, a display infinitely more vulgar than nakedness.

"No, no!" the priest said, aghast. "Put them inside!"

The Indian was perplexed. "What if I need to use him?"

"Then go behind a tree."

This suggestion struck the Indian as high absurdity. He howled with glee and spun around on a heel.

Another reason El Loco decided to come live at the mission was that he sensed in the grey-clad strangers a knowledge of necromancy and yearned to learn their tricks. He confided in Father Moreno that he believed he was attuned to the supernatural and that eventually he hoped to become a shaman. "Like you," he told the priest.

"I am not a shaman, Loco. I am a servant of God."

El Loco clapped his hands and danced a shuffle. "What's the difference?"

"A priest is chosen by Jesus Christ, the Son of God, to represent Him here on earth."

"Then I'll be a priest," the young man said.

"You have a wife?" Father Moreno asked.

"Oh, sure. Every man has a wife."

"Then you will bring her here to live with you?"

El Loco shook his head. "Maybe some day," he said.

"Why not now?"

"She has the baby." And when Father Moreno suggested he bring the child as well, El Loco said children were a damned nuisance and he thought the padres were smart not to have any.

"We want children. The more the better," the priest said. Whereupon the Indian shrugged as if to say, "Each to his own taste."

Father Moreno said, "We want to educate the children. We want to better their lives, to lead them into the path of righteousness."

Uncomfortable in argument, especially when not sure of his ground, the Indian said the real trouble was his wife's mother: she would have to come, too, and he did not want to live with her. Indeed, one of the reasons he had come to live at the Mission was to get away from the old bitch. "She is a coyote," he said.

"We want the women to come live here, too," Father Moreno said, and then, suddenly realizing that the statement might be misinterpreted, he went on quickly: "We want to teach them how to prepare and cook food. We want to teach them how to live the good life. And we want to teach them the ways of God."

El Loco either didn't understand or wasn't interested. At this point he uttered a string of unintelligible sounds and, to indicate that for him the matter was settled, broke into a tromping dance.

"You want your child to know many things?" the Priest asked.

Still dancing, the Indian said he was not certain the child was his. Others had been in the nest before him, he said.

"Well, I want you to do this for me," the priest said: "I want you to ask your wife to bring the baby and come here to live. We will build you a strong house and feed you and raise you all in the light of Jesus Christ."

Whether it was the reasoning, the offer of reward or the persistency of the argument that induced El Loco to accede, it would be hard to say. Not being the possessor of a strong intellect, he may finally have consented because his will to resist was exhausted. In any case, he said he would go and summon his wife if he could wear a soldier's helmet. Ignacio fulfilled this stipulation by snatching the helmet off Vincenti's fat head. And while the argument between the two soldiers waxed warm, El Loco, the leather hat askew on his banded head, strutted proudly off in the direction of the hot springs.

CHAPTER THREE

The Franciscans selected sites for their Missions with an eye for beauty, and the site Father Serra had chosen for the Mission San Simeon was an expanse of raised land from which one had a fine view down the valley of the ocean and the bay. To the north lay fertile river-bottom land in which grain could be grown. To the east the rounded bare hills rose gracefully into ever higher tiers to become lost in infinity. At hand was an inexhaustible supply of adobe for brickmaking and in the riverbed, besides gravel for walks and roads, a substantial thicket of tules for roofing.

By the time Father President Serra departed for the long trek to the Mission San Gabriel, work had begun on a chapel and living quarters, plans had been drawn for a guardhouse, a storehouse, a kitchen, a toolshed and a workshop to be constructed in a quadrangle sixty varas square. Besides olives, peach, and apricot, fig, pomegranate and grape seedlings had been planted in what would be the compound.

Father Serra's parting words were "You have made a good start, but remember it's baptisms we want."

The Father President had hardly passed from sight before Father Trujillo came to tell Father Moreno he had caught Pepito stealing chocolate.

"How do you know he was stealing it?" Father Moreno asked irritatedly.

"Well, he was eating it. We don't have an abundance, you know."

"Perhaps Father Serra gave it to him."

The younger priest's mouth drew up tight. He started to turn away, but he could not bring himself to leave without saying: "If I may say so, Father, you are spoiling that child."

"Now just a minute," Father Moreno said testily. "Let us understand each other. We're going to be living here together for some time and we might as well get one thing straight. That boy is my responsibility, and I'll bring him up as I see fit."

Later that afternoon, Father Moreno, ashamed of his display of choler, sought to make amends. He went to his brother priest, busy filling water jugs, and said he was going to the sea to take a bath. "Would you care to join me?"

They set out, going quickly according to the younger man's natural haste. As they proceeded Father Moreno questioned his companion and learned that he had been brought up in Cadiz; that his father had died when he was but a few months old; that his mother had worked as a seamstress; that he had been drawn to the priesthood because of his religious faith, and that he had joined the Franciscan Order rather than become a diocesan priest because the latter does not take the vow of poverty and usually remains near his home. "He serves the parish to which he is assigned, saying Mass, preaching, visiting the sick, marrying, baptising and burying the dead. I wanted none of that," the younger priest said. "It was not challenging enough for me. I wanted to go out into the world and carry the Word of God to the heathen and the ignorant."

"God has brought you to the right place."

"Missionaries have it the hardest, so the Heavenly rewards should be the greatest," Father Trujillo said.

"I joined the Order," Father Moreno said, "because I had an uncle, God rest his soul, who was a Franciscan. And I, too, wanted to go far to save souls rather than to save them at home. I suppose such notions are a concomitant of youth." The older man glanced at his companion's face for a reaction, found none. "I have lived long enough to learn that there is an inexhaustible supply of sin everywhere." And then, putting a hand on his companion's arm, he said, jokingly, "If you don't slow down you'll hasten us both into early graves."

Father Trujillo slowed his pace. "I'm sorry. I fear to misuse time. There is so much to be done."

Father Moreno stopped to remove a bit of gravel from a sandal. He squinted upward, his heavy skinned, stubbled face puckered against the direct rays of the sun. "The older I get," he said, "the less I seem to know." And then, as they went on: "When I was young everything was quite simple. There was right and there was wrong, and they were as easily recognizable as black and white. Now I have doubts about many things."

The younger priest shook his head admonishingly. "There is no place in the priesthood for doubt," he said.

"For example," Father Moreno went on, "I have begun to doubt whether it is possible to make Christians of savages. The heathens here will profess to understand and accept Christianity, but they will do so I'm afraid only because we feed them."

"Of all the people in the world, they need help."

"You forget the Lutherans," Father Moreno said jocularly; and when his companion did not indicate any appreciation of the jest, he added, "I would consider it a favor if you would at least smile at my jokes."

The younger man said: "To me it is not a joke. I don't see any excuse for Lutherans. Why don't they come out here and convert the heathen? Because they don't think these poor people are worth worrying about, that's why." He paused and, when no comment was forthcoming, went on: "I ask those Protestant gentlemen: If the Apostles had remained in their fatherland, sitting at home behind the stove, where would the world be today? Does Christ command: 'Go ye into all the world and preach the Gospel to every creature' include the Protestant preachers or does it not? If it does, why do they not obey?"

This youthful onslaught mildly amused Father Moreno. "Let us not waste time being intolerant of the Protestants," he said. "There's too much intolerance in the world as it is."

"I'm afraid tolerance for enemies of the Church is not one of my virtues," Father Trujillo said self-righteously.

They had been following the tule-fringed creek and now the tules ended and just ahead of them was the beach. The sun was at four o'clock and its rays bounced glitteringly off the myriad wavelets. "Out here," Father Moreno said, "you'll find that our most relentless and implacable enemy is loneliness—the hunger for spiritual warmth and companionship. The reason the Church sends two of us out here together is not so much because of the physical dangers involved, though they are considerable, but because of our failty in isolation. Removed from the companionship of his own kind, a civilized man, even a priest, may lose his balance."

"Loneliness I do not fear," Father Trujillo said. "My only fear is that I may fail to do God's will."

As the men approached the beach a flock of pelicans rose warily from the water's edge, their great wings flapping for altitude; then in fine formation they went into an effortless glide, riding the updraft of a swelling wave.

The older priest squatted to feel the water, but the wave receded. He followed it, only to be caught by the next one, which came in too quickly for him to escape. He stamped his wet sandaled feet, laughing and shaking his skirt. "Feels fine," he said, and began disrobing. His deeply tanned face, neck and hands were in sharp contrast to the white skin and black hair of his body. To avoid the embarrassment of looking at him, Father Trujillo pretended interest in a bevy of sand-pipers feeding at some distance down the beach. More than a dozen of the long-legged birds moved in unison with great rapidity, following an outgoing wave to poke their beaks hungrily into the draining sand.

The naked priest ran into the water and plunged through a swell just before it broke. He emerged floating on his back. "Come on in! Is very good!"

Father Trujillo looked furtively along the beach before beginning shyly to disrobe. Father Moreno swam out a way, using the breaststroke. Now he came back, caught a wave to his liking and rode it in. Father Trujillo's frail body looked bloodless; the basket of his ribs appeared all but empty, and there was a large birthmark on one breast. With an almost female display of modesty, he went to the water's edge and stuck in a toe, only to draw it out quickly, shudder-ing.

"There's nothing to be afraid of," Father Moreno hollered, and dove into another swell.

The younger man held his breath, scooped some water in his hands and rubbed it over his arms and chest. Then he ventured out a few paces until the water came up to his knees; there he turned his back to the waves and squatted down. Father Moreno saw a swell gathering behind his companion, but perversity prevented his warning him. In this instance he thought it was far more entertaining to let nature take its course than to thwart it. When the oncoming wall of water broke over him, Father Trujillo was swallowed up, "as" he said later "was Jonah by the whale." Rolled onto the sand, he scrambled blindly, unsteadily to his feet, stood coughing and spitting and blinking his sand-filled eyes.

Father Moreno, striding out of the water, went into a spasm of coughing to stifle his laughter. "You have to watch the swells," he cautioned. "They're very treacherous."

When they had dried themselves and dressed, they set out for "home", walking a way along the beach looking for shells.

Back in the reed-and-mud hut which had been erected as a tem-porary shelter, Father Moreno asked his companion: "What would you say to a dram of wine?" and reached under a pack for a bota. "Let us drink to the success of Mission San Simeon."

"Not for me, thank you," Father Trujillo said. "I take wine only at Communion."

The older man paused, surprised. "No wine?" he asked,

disappointed. "Oh, come now," he went on, "you're not going to force me to drink alone?" He proferred the bota to Father Trujillo who hesitantly, reluctantly accepted it. Father Moreno said, "May our Heavenly Father bless us all." When it came his turn some of the wine ran down his considerable chin and lodged in his whiskers. In wiping his face with his hand, the stubble of his beard made a rasping sound. He smacked his large lips. "Be it not abused," he said, "wine is a good friend," and added, "although I must say, moderation is the least of the virtues.

Father Trujillo said, "I confess I am not much of a drinker. Wine has a tendency to go to my head."

"Precisely why it is so rewarding. It lifts the spirit, renews the vigor and tunes one in with the universe. To me it is over-scrupulous to deny oneself this pleasure on moral grounds. If you do not like the taste or the effect, that is understandable. But if a man abstains because he believes it is wrong, ah, I sorrow for him."

"My only pleasure comes from doing God's will," Father Trujillo said. "Otherwise pleasure makes me feel guilty."

"In this life and out here especially, there is little opportunity for pleasure. One should seize it when he can." Father Moreno squeezed the goatskin bag, squirted some more into his mouth.

Father Trujillo said, "I wish I could have your lighthearted attitude toward life."

"It comes with age."

"You even seem to take the rules of the Church lightly."

"The rules of the Church are calculated to remind us of our ecclesiastical obligations. Out here we don't need to be reminded."

"The rules are ordinations of God, like the ten commandments."

"So we are taught." Father Moreno looked askance at his companion. "I'm no heretic, but as I grow older I find that truth is several sided, depending on the point of view."

"I don't understand."

"What may be truthful to you may not be to me."

Not wanting to pursue such dangerous thoughts, the younger priest excused himself, saying, "I'll go say my office," and ducked out.

As Father Moreno gazed at the doorway through which his fellow priest had gone, he thought: *Why do I take such delight in trying to shock him out of his rigidity?*

Pepito appeared in the doorway.

26

"Is *bueno* I go fishing with Ignacio, Father?"

"Just a minute." the priest said. "What's this I hear about you stealing chocolate?" And while the boy, taken aback, fumbled in his mind for an excuse, the man went on: "That's one thing I will not condone—you stealing. Understand?"

"Vincenti took some, too."

"I don't care who else took some. Not only did you steal, you made it worse by lying to Father Trujillo about it. Why did you tell him I gave you permission?"

The boy hung his head.

"If I catch you stealing or lying again I'll wash my hands of you. Do you hear me?" But even as Pepito nodded, the priest realized this was an empty threat: he would do nothing of the kind. "Go ahead," he said. "Be sure you're back before nightfall."

From a mass of rocks which jutted out into the bay Ignacio and Pepito cast their lines. For a time, seated on a boulder, they devoted themselves to the business at hand. Only the swells spewing onto the rocks and the occasional screech of a gull disturbed the silence. Eventually Ignacio spoke: "What's this about you wanting to be a priest when you grow up?"

"Maybe I will. Maybe I won't. I don't know."

"Do you believe all that about Jesus Christ being born of a virgin, the Son of God?"

"Sure, I believe it. I believe in the Father, the Son and the Holy Ghost. Don't you?"

"Would you mind telling me what is a Holy Ghost?"

The boy hesitated. "I don't know. He's the Holy Ghost, that's all. Father Georgio says He's in all of us."

Ignacio pulled in his line and cast it out again. "How old are you?"

"Be thirteen pretty soon."

"You're too young to know what being a priest means."

"It means I'll never get married. I know that."

"It means you can't have anything to do with women. It means you'll go through life being a beggar. It means you'll never be able to do what you want to do."

"I'd like to be a priest if I could be like Father Georgio," the boy said. "Everybody looks up to him."

27

"Father Georgio's a good man. But when you're a priest you've got to be good. That's the whole trouble." Ignacio's line tightened and he devoted his attention to it. "You don't believe that Jesus was the son of God, do you? Or that his mother was a virgin?"

"Of course. That is what the Bible says."

"Well, don't believe the Bible. It's full of a lot of fairy tales." He brought in a fair sized corvina. "I suppose you believe that one good turn deserves another?"

"Sure."

"Then you've never heard the story of the ungrateful alligator?" The boy shook his head. "No."

"Well, there was this alligator lying on his back beside the river trying to turn himself over so that he could get back into the water, but paw the air as he did, he was unable to do so. When he was all but exhausted a man came along and, seeing his plight, turned him over. The weakened alligator asked the man to carry him to the water, which the man did; whereupon the alligator grabbed the man with his claws and said, 'I'm hungry. I'm going to eat you!' 'But,' the man said, aghast, 'I saved your life! One good turn deserves another.' 'That's not the way it is at all,' said the alligator. 'In this world it's dog eat dog. We'll just ask the burro coming yonder. Good afternoon brother burro,' he said. 'Is it true that one good turn deserves another?' 'Not at all,' said the burro. 'When I was young I served my masters well. I carried their burdens through fair weather and foul. Now that I'm old they have turned me out to die.' 'You see,' said the alligator to the man, 'it is just as I said. Now I am going to eat you.' 'One minute,' said the man. 'Here comes an ox. Let us ask him. Tell me, brother ox, do you believe that a good turn should be repaid with a bad?' 'Oh, yes, it is true,' said the ox. 'When I was young I ploughed the fields for my masters. Now that I am old they have cut off my horns and are fattening me up to butcher me.' 'Does that satisfy you?' asked the alligator. 'Wait!' the man pleaded. 'Here comes a coyote. If he says the same as the other then this world is not fit to live in and you may eat me.' And the man said, 'Good afternoon, brother coyote. Isn't it true that one good turn deserves another?' Said the coyote: 'I cannot hear for the noise of the running water.' So the alligator brought the man ashore and he repeated the question. 'That depends,' the coyote said. 'Why do you want to know?' and the man explained the situation, saying that having saved the alligator's life the alligator now wanted to eat him. 'Well,' the coyote said, 'I can't render judgement until I see just how the alligator was lying.' So the alligator lay down and rolled onto his back as he was when the man came upon him. At that point the coyote said to the man, 'Now leave the ingrate there to die.'

"'How can I ever repay you?' the man asked the coyote. 'Well, you might bring me a couple of chickens.' said the coyote. 'I'm awful fond of chickens.' 'Come to my house,' the man said, 'and you may have as many as you like.' 'I don't trust the dogs at your house,' the coyote said. 'Bring the chickens here.' So the man went away and came back with a sack over a shoulder. 'How will you like these?—one at a time or all together?'' the man asked, unshouldering the sack. 'Turn them all loose,' the coyote said. 'I'll enjoy running them down.' Whereupon the man opened the sack and out came two dogs which forthwith took out after the coyote. The coyote managed to get up on a ledge out of the dogs' reach and he said to the man, 'That was a mean trick, after all I did for you. I'll never do another good turn as long as I live.'

"So you see, Pepito," Ignacio concluded, "that's the way of this world. No matter what the padres say, it's dog eat dog and the Devil take the hindmost."

Pepito blinked his eyes. "What is an alligator?" he asked.

CHAPTER FOUR

El Loco returned to the Mission toward nightfall, his face bearing scratches. Referring to the lacerations, Father Moreno asked, "Your wife?"

"No. Her mother, the *chauhuistle*." El Loco spat with disgust. "She is poisonous."

"Your wife—is she coming?"

The young man shook his head in that emphatic, mocking way of his. "The baby is sick," he said unconcernedly. "She no come. She is afraid."

"What of?"

El Loco did not like being pressed. He let it be known that he was through with his wife and her bitch-dog of a mother. He said the old woman was the cause of all his troubles, past and present, and that she was a skunk that stank up every place she went. He said she had a bite like a baracuda and was forever sucking his blood and that he was a new man now that he was rid of her.

"Won't your wife come without her mother?" the priest asked, unaware it was the native custom that when a man paired with a woman he also took on her unattached sisters and, if widowed, her mother as well.

El Loco shook his head again. "Her mother rules her," he said. "She has no mind of her own."

"Who is the chief in your house?"

El Loco said he was, of course. "The man is always chief."

"Then simply demand that your wife join you."

"I get another wife," El Loco said.

"God does not approve of a man having more than one wife," the priest said.

"Then I am sorry for God," the Indian said. "One woman no forage enough to feed a man. Anyway," he added proudly, "I cannot be bothered with those stupid women."

30

Within a ten-mile radius of the Mission were scattered several villages, called by the Spaniards *rancherias*, the inhabitants of which generally were hostile to one another. Mutual distrust had been ingrained in the Californians' psyches for centuries, so that when the padres came preaching the message of Jesus Christ: "Love thy neighbor. Do unto others as you would have them do unto you," the Californians thought they must be crazy. El Loco challenged the philosophy, pointing out that he and his people had the only hot springs in the area; and he said if he and his people did not keep a sharp lookout they could get massacred for them.

"Is that the way you got the springs?" Father Moreno asked.

"Sure." Then El Loco said, "We kill them or they kill us," and put up his hands in a gesture of hopelessness, as if to say, "It is the way of this world."

"Did it ever occur to you to permit everyone to use the hot springs?" the priest asked. "Don't you know that if you treat your neighbors as brothers, they will so treat you?"

"You don't know the sonsofbitches," the Californian said, or words to that effect.

To avoid a possible conflict, the padres decided to invite the inhabitants of one *rancheria* at a time to visit the Mission, and their first invitation went to the people of El Loco's village. The lure they used was food. About twenty came. To Father Moreno's disappointment, El Loco's wife was not among them. Neither was his mother-in-law. With the food the priests served up a goodly portion of Christian doctrine. Most of the Indians went to sleep during the ceremony of the Mass, and they got another nap while Father Trujillo preached a sermon on brotherhood. The only time the priest had their complete attention was when he beat himself on the chest with a rock to drive out the devils. By the time the psalm-singing began most of the Indians had wandered off, homeward bound.

"They don't understand the language," Father Trujillo said to explain their disinterest. The two priests were in the *cocina* with Pepito, cleaning up. El Loco was seated in a corner blowing on a wooden whistle.

"I think they were bored," Father Moreno said, adding, "I guess religion isn't very entertaining. These people live such easy going lives their only interest is in having a good time. Isn't that right, Loco?"

El Loco stopped whistling. His expression was a query. Father Moreno resorted to sign language: "All you and your people want to

31

do is have a good time. Is that not so?"

El Loco nodded and laughed. "Doesn't everyone?"

Father Trujillo said, "Everything is a joke to El Loco."

Father Moreno said, "It's not going to be easy to indoctrinate these people. We've got to find ways to make Christianity fun." And he asked El Loco what they could do to attract Californians to the Mission.

The Californian said his people liked to eat and dance. He said that periodically, usually during a time of plenty such as when the cactus fruit is ripe, they had group parties. Participants painted their bodies in many colors. There was music from gourds containing pebbles, from drums and from strings of small bones which made a noise like castanets. Throughout the night people sang and danced, glutted themselves and fornicated. There might be footraces and other athletic contests.

When this had been translated for benefit of Father Trujillo he, somewhat embarrassed, said, "Well, at least we can have the singing and the dancing, the feasting and the athletic contests."

To which Father Moreno added: "Doubtless the fornication will take care of itself."

Next morning Father Moreno persuaded El Loco to help with the brickmaking. His job was to tromp the mud to the proper consistency. His pale-soled big feet made a sucking sound as he moved them up and down in the adobe. He went about the work with a light heart, making of it a dance. Suddenly he stopped and his good humor vanished. His attention was arrested by the sight of a short, thin, wizened woman coming up the path from the arroyo. He became greatly agitated. "The *chauhuistle*!" he cried, in much the way he might have announced an earthquake.

Father Moreno looked up to see the woman striding aggressively toward them, her fore and aft deerskin aprons snapping against her knotted knees. "Who is it?" the priest asked.

"My wife's mother." El Loco spat to show his disgust, stepped out of the mud, and picked up a stone with which to defend himself.

"Why, Loco, you're not afraid of *her*! She's hardly as big as a bug."

"She got poison tongue, like rattlesnake."

By now the little woman, whom the priests would come to call

Suegra which means mother-in-law, was gesticulating angrily and it was quite clear that the object of her ire was El Loco. As she approached Father Moreno stood up, bowed, and said, "Welcome, seniorita," but she swept past him without acknowledging his greeting and yapped at El Loco: "Where have you been, you good-for-nothing worm?"

El Loco drew the stone back threateningly. "What business is it of yours?"

"You're never where you're needed. Your child is deathly sick."

"What's the matter with her?"

"What do you care what's the matter with her. She's hot. She's burning up. I don't know what's the matter with her."

"How about Birdwing, the medicine man?—Can't he cure her?"

"That old fart!—He couldn't cure a mosquito bite."

"Well, if he can't, what can I do?"

"You can come home. You can forage some food."

Father Moreno saw in the situation a chance to demonstrate the healing powers of God. He seized the opportunity. "We will go and see if we cannot help the child," he said. "We will take food." And he called to Father Trujillo, laying brick to form the chapel: "God has sent this woman to us! Let us drop everything and go at once!"

With Falco as guard and Suegra as guide, they set out, following a path which cut across a field of mustard and ran along the rocky riverbed. Breathing hard as they hastened, Father Moreno said, "I warn you, Salvatore: we're going to have to compete with the *hechicero*, the witch-doctor. They're the bane of a missionary's life. We had the Devil's own time with them in the Sierra Gordo and at Santa Gertrudas. They don't like us because we put them out of business."

"I wonder how one becomes a *hechicero*?"

"Only the Devil knows. As a rule they're old men, and it helps if they have some physical abnormality. A hunchback, say. You've noticed that Californians are beardless; in fact, if you except the head, neither men nor women as a rule have any hair on their bodies. But every now and then, perhaps one in a hundred, a man will have some facial hair, sort of a goatee; and whenever this happens his peers will believe he has been touched by the gods." Father Moreno shrugged. "He becomes a *hechicero*, a shaman."

Father Trujillo snorted.

The older priest went on: "They claim to be able to foretell the

33

future, change the weather, avert catastrophes, thwart their enemies and inflict or cure disease."

"And the people believe them?"

"They're afraid not to."

"How stupid!"

"Oh, some have a knowledge of medicinal herbs and they probably effect an occasional cure. But in the main they are unmitigated liars. Say a sick person dies. The shaman will claim, and everyone will believe, that he purposely willed the person to die because of some wrong he committed. If the patient recovers, the shaman will noisily take credit for the cure. And their fearful listeners do not dare dispute them."

"I suppose they are handsomely rewarded for their services?"

"They get anything they want in the way of food and drink and use the women as they wish. The women are afraid to deny them self-gratification."

Father Trujillo was incensed. "They're agents of the Devil! We'll have to show them up for what they are!"

"We can't do it overnight. It'll have to come slowly, through education. Meanwhile, the one thing we must *not* do is treat them with contempt. They can do us much harm."

"How do you propose we negate them?"

"The only way we can do it is with love: Christianity's great strength. If there is a shaman involved with the sick child—and it is almost a certainty there will be—we're going to treat him with great respect. We're going to kill him with kindness."

Presently they came in sight of a cluster of reed-and-mud huts set amongst sycamore and cottonwood trees. Steam rose from several springs and their overflow rattled down into the otherwise dry riverbed and disappeared into the sand. A group of solemn-faced natives gathered to watch as Suegra and the Spaniards advanced. One of them, an old man singularly short of stature, began an harangue, shouting and slapping his thin, bare thighs. He wore the shaman's badge of office—a necklace of human hair—but otherwise was unadorned. Most of his teeth were missing: one of the reasons many of the words he uttered were incomprehensible.

While Father Moreno was eager to administer to the sick child and thereby demonstrate the power of Almighty God, he made no attempt to interrupt the spokesman. So the little old man droned on and one, saying what he had to say. Eventually he ran out of words and stood chewing his gums, awaiting a response. Using sign language to supplement his meager Chumash, Father Moreno said how happy he and his companions were to be so well received. He said they had come at the behest of Suegra to administer to a sick child. And he asked of the shaman—"What is your name, sir?"

"I am called Birdwing."

"Would you, Senor Birdwing, come and assist us in restoring the health of the child?"

The old man was surprised and flattered by the invitation and readily agreed, not disclosing that he had already used on the patient to no avail such powers as he possessed.

With Suegra and the shaman leading the way, the priests proceeded to a wickiup of willows driven into the ground, its chinks plastered with adobe. It required but a few hours for a man and a woman to erect such an abode, and when after a time it became uninhabitable due to the multiplicity of vermin the householders would burn it and build another.

Whereas the shaman and Suegra merely had to bend over to pass through the small entrance, the priests had to go in on hands and knees. El Loco's wife sat cross-legged before a smouldering fire, a baby in her arms. She was quite young, hardly in her teens, and despite the anxiety in her expression and the pigments on her face and hair, quite pretty. Her skin was not as dark as others of her race and her nose was exceptional in that it was straight and well proportioned. The hut's furnishings were few. Baskets hung from fishbone hooks. On the dirt floor were a stone mortar and pestle for grinding acorns and chia seeds, and a stack of abalone shells. Two declivities for sleeping had been scraped in the earth and filled with grasses.

The baby, but a few weeks old, was breathing with difficulty. Father Moreno put out his hands to take the child, but the mother drew away. Suegra scolded her daughter and, snatching the baby, tendered her to the priest. The baby burst out crying. Birdwing began mumbo-jumboing and making faces. Father Moreno asked for water and Suegra used a shell to dip some from a basked. The priest blessed it and applied a few drops to the child's hot head, saying, "I baptize thee Maria Magdelena, for the Mother of Jesus, in the name of the Father and the Son and the Holy Spirit," raising his voice against the baby's wailing and Birdwing's wierd incantations. Then, as a ploy to silence the shaman, Father Moreno offered him the crying infant, indicating that he should work his magic on her. The old man promptly sat down cross-legged, the child on his naked thighs and, spitting on his hands, began massaging her chest and legs, it being generally believed that with his saliva a shaman could cure any ailment.

To the surprise of everyone, especially Birdwing, the baby stopped crying, whereupon the shaman returned her triumphantly to Father Moreno, indicating that he had saved her life. Babe in arms, the priest knelt and began to pray, beggin Mary, Virgin and Queen of Angels, tower of health and comforter of the afflicted, to intercede in the baby's behalf.

It was a mighty struggle, this contest between the exorcists, the Christian and the barbarian. In it were entwined on the one side the mysticism man has conjured to substitute for his ignorance and on the other man's yearning for redemption. An observer might have thought that the success or failure of the Mission was dependent on its outcome, and indeed in a very real sense it was Christianity's first crucial test at San Simeon.

It is unthinkable, Father Moreno thought, *that God in His infinite wisdom will allow the child to die and thereby turn His back on a petition that means so much to the Mission.*

The priest was still leaning into prayer with all his spiritual strength, when the shaman, in an effort to reassert himself, began stomping his feet in what he deemed a dance. The dust his feet raised and the odor of unwashed bodies in those close confines made breathing both difficult and unplesant, and Father Moreno interrupted his prayer to request permission to take the baby outside. The mother said nothing; she seemed mesmerized. But Suegra said it would be all right, and everyone went out into the stark sunshine. There, surrounded by gaping natives, Father Moreno knelt, babe in arms, and continued his prayer. And so earnest was he, so pressing in his plea that it seemed by his very zeal the child would be saved.

Before leaving the baby's fate in God's hands, Father Moreno flattered Birdwing and lauded him to the other Californians. The priest also gave him a necklace of large beads and told him: "You could become a very powerful person if you learned the ways of God." And once they were out of hearing he said to Father Trujillo: "If we can convert that old devil we'll have eliminated a powerful obstacle."

Coming into the cocina for breakfast the next morning, Father Trujillo said to Father Moreno, who had all but finished his repast: "I had a manifestation last night. God came and told me the child will live."

"Let's hope it was not a dream," Father Moreno said, stuffing the last half of a *tortilla* into his mouth. Chewing, he went on: "If we're going to have bread we've got to get the wheat into the ground before the rains come." He drained his cup of chocolate, took out his snuff-box and sniffed a pinch of tobacco, doing so with exaggerated enjoyment, contrarily pleased that Father Trujillo did not approve of the habit. He then picked up two leathern buckets, went out into the early morning and was surprised to see Birdwing come limping through the main gate. He hurried to welcome the old man.

"Some one has put the curse on me," the shaman said, the words coming indistinct from his toothless mouth. "I got this bad leg," he went on, feeling his left knee. "Reckon your God can cure it?"

"Why, yes. I'm sure he can."

"It's right here," the old man said, raising and patting his knee.

Father Moreno seated the shaman on the bench beside the chapel and examined the gnarled joint. "I think if you stay off it for a while—give it a rest, it'll be all right," he told him. "Stay here with us and let God get at it."

The old man thought that would be fine. "Here maybe the curse can't reach me," he said.

Father Moreno escorted him to the *cocina* and left him with Father Trujillo.

Passing the barrack on his way to the granary, the older priest saw Pepito lying on a bunk watching the soldiers play cards. Ignacio was shuffling.

"When I enlisted," Falco was saying, "they told me they wanted me to populate the country."

"How can you populate without women?"

"Anza brought a batch to San Gabriel Mission," Pedro said.

"A lot of good that does us."

Falco said, "They also promised they would give us land."

"How much you want?" Ignacio asked. "Couple of thousand *varas*? Take as many as you like."

"Well, well," Pedro said mockingly, "a landowner, eh? Proud to know you, Don Senor."

"Let's see," Ignacio said, counting on his fingers "the taxes are one guilder a *vara*. That'll be two thousand guilders. I'm the tax collector. Pay me."

37

"Deal the cards," Falco said.

Father Moreno thought that these men had left their habitats to go off into limbo because of a curious nonconformity in their characters. They were wanderers, seekers of they knew not what, masculine as profanity, yet foolishly romantic runners-away from reality. And watching and listening to them, the priest thought they, like the vast majority of mankind, were prisoners of their own ignorance. From his point of view they were as dangerous as they were useful. It was almost too much to hope that they would not make trouble with their genitals.

"Pepito!"

The boy quickly got to his feet, and the soliders all turned to look at Father Moreno standing in the doorway. "Yes Father?"

"There's work to do. Here—take these buckets. And you—"without rancor to the soldiers,"—the Lord needs you to make bricks."

The boy and the missionary walked together in silence for a few paces while the priest wrestled with the problem of how most effectively to warn the child against the evils about him. He rejected several ideas as being pontifical, obscure or not wholly true, and finally as they came up to the storehouse said, "If you expect to go into the priesthood, Pepito, I suggest you not fill your head with such nonsense as card games." He started to say that soldiers were a bad influence, but thought better of it. After all, the soldiers were a part of their social structure; the boy would have to live with them. Furthermore there was no way to protect the boy from evil; he would have to learn the bad with the good.

"We have neglected your lessons of late," the priest said. "Do you remember how to spell evil?"

"*D - i - a - b - l - o.*"

"And good?"

"*D - i - o - s.*"

"Very good."

The padre let it go at that. He picked up a bucket, filled it with grain, and they went into the field adjoining the stockade to the south.

Father Moreno tucked the hem of his habit into his waistcord so that the skirt would not impede his work. He set Pepito to hoeing ahead of him and himself went about the task of planting the seed with great meticulousness. As one by one, he poked them into the soil, he said, "We have to give every grain a chance to grow. Next spring, praise God, we will have much corn."

Man and boy had been engaged thus for some time when there hove into view El Loco's wife and her mother. The younger woman was carrying the baby on her back in a basket suspended from her forehead, and in a like basket Suegra was carrying their possessions. Father Moreno hurried to greet them. They told him that during the night the baby's illness had disappeared. It was a miracle brought about, they were convinced, by the intercession of the padres. The overjoyed priest had the two women kneel at once and together they thanked God for the "deliverance."

Father Moreno sent Pepito to summon El Loco and when he came said to him: "Your family has come to live with us. They have come because they want to live under God's protection."

El Loco shrugged to divest himself of any responsibility. He said that, if the priests took the old woman in, they and God would be sorry. Whereupon his mother-in-law screamed spit-spewed insults upon him and his ancestors for several hundred generations. He was, she screamed, a short-horned hoot-owl, the issue of an eel and a jellyfish that had been spawned in excrement. While Father Moreno did not understand all of the words she uttered, no one could have mistaken the venom with which she spoke them. When finally the priest was able to silence her he told El Loco: "We will build a house here for you, your wife and your child, so that you may live in a Christian harmony. As for your wife's mother, she will have a place of her own and I shall see to it that she does not interfere with your life."

When this was explained to the older woman she again became vituperative, vowing she would not be separated from her daughter and grandchild. And when Father Moreno pointed out that it was obvious she and El Loco could not live happily together, Suegra said it was all his fault, that he was a no-good dog who, though he has women at home, poked around elsewhere.

El Loco countered by saying he would rather live with a skunk than Suegra. "A rattlesnake's tongue is not so poisonous," he said. Father Moreno promised the old woman she would have charge of the kitchen, which mollified her, and for the nonce the argument ended.

Father Moreno's first concern was to clothe El Loco's wife, whom he named Consuelo. The apron she wore did not always hide her crotch and she wore nothing over her beautifully proportioned breasts. The priest took the two women to his temporary quarters and fashioned dresses for them. In cut, the garments were very like the habits worn by the missionaries: hemmed pieces of cloth with holes for head and arms. Consuelo was delighted with her dress but quickly became concerned as to how, while wearing it, she could feed her baby. To make this possible without removing the garment, Father Moreno slit an opening from the neckline and then fastened it with a pin. Consuelo fashioned a belt of deerskin and wore it about her waist in imitation of the padres, but her less vain mother was content to let her sacklike covering hang loose from her skinny shoulders. Although Father Moreno thought he was minimizing Consuelo's physical attractions by covering them, in fact she was more seductive in the dress than she had been all but naked.

"Now that you have come to live in God's way," the priest said to Consuelo, "I want you to wash that paste off your face and clean your hair. I think somewhere under all that is a pretty girl."

Though it must have cost her much, Consuelo did as Father Moreno proposed. And when her copper-black hair had dried in the sun, he gave her a hairbrush and taught her to use it and to tie the hair at the nape. This done, hair brushed back and tied with a bit of ribbon, brown face scrubbed clean, teeth gleaming, she was quite pretty indeed. Moreover there was inate artistry in her carriage, a natural grace and rhythm. She had her share of pride and vanity, and it was fascinating to watch her use her charms instinctively, as a civilized woman does, to gain her ends.

Consuelo's personality complimented her comeliness. In her feminine way she was as vivacious and unpredictable and guileless as El Loco. Her naivete and unaffectedness cut through the civilized restraints of the padres and frequently left them aghast. She was eager to learn Spanish and was comparatively quick to pick it up. Father Trujillo was her teacher and he was sometimes hard put to answer her penetrating and embarrassing questions.

"Have you seen God?" she asked him suddenly one day. And when he said no, she wanted to know how then he knew God existed. On one occasion she asked why stealing is a sin, and on another, pointing to Father Trujillo's crotch, asked, "How do you call that?"

She was intrigued by Father Trujillo because of his blue eyes. There was a legend among her people that the gods, including Chinigchinich, were blue-eyed, and she believed the priest had magical powers. Just as El Loco had become a disciple of Father Moreno, so Consuelo became a slave to Father Trujillo. As soon as her initial shyness and awe wore off she proved to be impulsive and brash and was not at all reticent about showing her infatuation for him. While her overt attentions sometimes embarrassed him, he was secretly pleased that she looked upon him as being sanctified.

This day she came to his cell with his laundered vestments. When he opened the door she started to enter. He reacted with vexation and embarrassment. "No, no!" he said. "You mustn't!" and stuck his head outside to see if anyone was watching. When he took the laundry she put a hand on his genitals.

"I take him," she said.

Father Trujillo jumped back. "We priests do not do that!" he said. "Now you go!"

"How you have babies?"

"We don't! God does not want us to have children. We are priests. Everyone is our child. Now you go on."

Instead of obeying, she pushed inside and rubbed herself against him, suggested with shocking candor that she be allowed to come in and join him in sexual intercourse. He reacted with vexation and embarrassment. "No, no, no!" he whispered, as if she had slapped him.

"Blue eyes!" she said coaxingly.

He resisted her with strength and indignation. "Stop it!—"

"Mmmm," she muttered, pursing her lips to kiss him.

He thrust her outside and slammed the door.

Before turning away, Consuelo stood for a moment snickering at his confusion. Later he said to Father Moreno: "I'm afraid we have created a problem in Consuelo."

"How is that?"

"We have made her so attractive that the soldiers are going to want her."

Father Moreno pursed his lips thoughtfully. "Perhaps one will want to marry her."

"But she is already married to El Loco."

"Not in the Church."

CHAPTER FIVE

The first few months the priests and soldiers were occupied raising permanent shelters for themselves: a temporary chapel and a kitchen. These were built of adobe bricks with roofs of thatched tules and were surrounded by a stockade of tall posts set close together. A corral was constructed adjoining the stockade. Father Trujillo discovered a deposit of lime and the interiors of the structures were whitewashed to help dilute the darkness and discourage insects. El Loco and Consuelo built a wickiup for themselves outside the stockade, and the padres built Suegra a hut next to the kitchen. The kitchen was equipped with a copper pan, a copper pot in which to prepare chocolate, several other pots made of clay, a small spit, and some cow bladders containing fat and other comestibles.

Log benches were installed in the chapel and yucca-frond mats covered the aisle. The altar was draped with richly galloon silk. The chalices, the ciboria, the monstrances, the censers, the crucifixes, the altar bells and the candlesticks were all of silver; surplices, chasubles, robes and humerales were of fine linen and lace and shot through with threads of gold: finery designed to put the natives in awe of the Almighty.

As word spread that Consuelo's baby had been cured by the magic of the missionaries, other Indians with a variety of ailments came to the Mission from various *rancherias*. All were treated with deliberate kindness as a persuasion for them to remain, and mud-and-tule huts were built for them outside the stockade. Thus did the community grow.

In the beginning water was brought to the Mission from the nearest source, a spring about half a mile up San Juan Creek. It was carried by hand in leather buckets or watertight baskets woven of cactus fibres. But after the grapevines and fruit trees were planted the need for water became so acute that Father Trujillo undertook to engineer a flume of hollowed-out logs by which water could be brought into the compound. While there was a downward slope from the spring to the Mission, it was interrupted at the source by an outcropping of granite, and to overcome this obstacle it was necessary to blast an opening through it.

Before setting off the charge of gunpowder, Father Moreno, to avoid frightening the Indians, explained to them what was about to take place. To his dismay they were opposed to it. They were afraid, they protested, that such a blast might destroy the spring, on which their lives depended. It could even bring about an earthquake, the most fearful of all the hazards man was subject to.

Father Moreno used his most persuasive tones to reassure them. He said that such a small detonation as was planned could not possibly damage the spring; on the contrary, it would improve it. And as for it causing an earthquake, that was beyond the bounds of reason.

But the natives remained unconvinced. El Loco told the priests that if the ground were disturbed, God would become angry and "Every time we make God angry he shakes the mountains."

"But God is already angry, because the spring is not serving His church," Father Moreno said. "Think of it this way," he went on, trying to simplify his argument in terms of natives could understand: "God has a toothache. You all know how painful a sore tooth can be. This spring is God's toothache, and the only way we can relieve His pain is to blow this rock away."

Still the Indians were opposed. They shook their heads and muttered among themselves, and Birdwing, the withered old shaman, said, "It will put a curse on us."

Unable to allay their apprehensions, Father Moreno said he was sorry but he and Father Trujillo would go ahead and do God's will. Whereupon the Indians, lead by El Loco, headed for higher ground where they could watch but would be safe from the consequences.

Using a crowbar, the priests managed to hollow out a cavity in the granite; into this Father Trujillo poured a gourdful of gunpowder and topped it with a rock. A cord smeared with resin served as a fuse. As Father Trujillo lit this, Father Moreno closed his eyes for a hasty prayer, asking God not to let the explosion cause the earth to tremble.

The explosion sent rock fragments whining through the air and the natives skurrying. It took a second blast to effect an adequate opening. A segment of flume was affixed therein and Father Trujillo started the water flowing through the system. As they followed its

43

course toward the Mission, Father Moreno congratulated his companion. "You have wrought a miracle," he said. "We'll have water enough to bathe."

Father Moreno's Journal: *The daily pattern of life of unbaptized Californians runs like this: In the morning they go searching for food. In the evening, when their bellies are full, they lie down to sleep or sit together talking and joking until they cannot think of anything more to say. Their chatter is mainly about food. Curiously, although the sexual act is very important to them, they do not talk much about it. They will work only if, like trained seals, they are rewarded with food. When the need arises the males make bows and arrows and the females make baskets and aprons; otherwise they are not productive. It never occurs to them to save anything for the morrow. Thus when we want them to work in the fields to produce food for the future—four, five or six moons hence—they consider the proposal absurd. When the Californians can be coerced to work they have to be closely supervised. The more of them there are working together, the less each does. And it is no use telling them how a job should be done; one has to show them down to the smallest detail and then watch to see that they do it properly. Those who consent to labor at anything do so only in spurts. While generally strong physically, they seem incapable of sustained concentration and are easily distracted; at unlikely times they will cease whatever they are doing to take a nap or go fishing. And if we try to punish them for not working they feign illness. It is remarkable when there is work to be done how many claim to be ill, then show up hale and hardy come Sunday, when we have meat.*

I do the ploughing. The plough is an iron sleeve tapered at one end with a wooden shaft. It is drawn by an ox. After the soil has been turned over, furrows are hoed and into the sides of the furrows seeds are pressed, one at a time because they are so precious. The same system is used for planting corn, beans, garbanzos, squash, pumpkins and melons. Wheat we sow. Once a week throughout the growing season water is run through the furrows. To ensure a crop, birds, particularly crows, have to be kept away, but worse even than the birds are the mice which, during the night, dig up and dine on the precious seeds. What we wouldn't give for a cat or two! The soil is absolutely marvelous. I do believe anything can grow here, including hopefully, goodness. . .

CHAPTER SIX

A year has passed since you last visited us here at San Simeon, Father Moreno wrote to Father President Junipero Serra *and I am happy to report the progress. We have brought into the vineyard, as of yesterday, forty-seven souls, all gleaned from Satan's overgrown weedpatch and baptized in the name of our Savior. And this is only the beginning. As you know, conversions accelerate; one neophyte attracts another. There have been four births and as yet no deaths. The most recent birth occured this week. The baby was the mother's first child. The mother is only thirteen. As a rule these women have children with the ease of cows; they don't require help. But this young lady, converted recently, would have died, I believe, had we not assisted her. Fortunately I had some experience in this miracle in the Sierro Gorda and know what to do. The native women are little help; about all they do is utter encouragement or poke fun. The baby, born backwards, was finally brought into the light of day and is a lusty-lunged addition to our flock. We took the liberty of naming him Junipero, after you Dear Father President, and your patron, the beloved companion of Saint Francis.*

Our completed structures include a small guest apartment and I pray that you will come and honor us with your presence when you can. Our first crop of grain amounted to six hundred and twelve fanagas, which we think is excellent; and next year we should be able to double it. The stock are multiplying. We have three new calves this month, six lambs and at least two of our mares are pregnant.

Now permit me, please to speak of our deficiencies. We need many things, Dear Father—chocolate and prepared wax and table oil, cloth and wicks and twine and rosaries and purificators and paper for writing and refined brandy and beads. We are badly in need of vestments. If we are going to do God's work—and the King's—we should impress the natives favorably. As it is, our habits are ragged, and as for underclothing—for shame! we have none.

46

All of these things are vital in our struggle to convert the natives, and of course all are obtainable in Mexico for dinero. *Unfortunately we have no surpluses to trade for them and to date we have received nothing from the Pious Fund. We religious have nothing but the cloth on our frames, our breviaries, our crucifixes and our faiths, and these, as you know, buy little in the market place. And while I am on the insistent subject, would you please use your great influence to intercede with proper authorities on behalf of the poor soldiers stationed here. Their wages are long overdue. They are under the impression, not so far fetched I think, that they have been sent out here and forgotten.*

Until we can build our own looms we need not only cloth but blankets. Indeed, we should have blankets and clothing for all of the converts and neophytes. Every six months, until we ran out, the neophytes were given fresh garments. By now, of course, they are beginning to look like scare-crows. Some of the men have a way of losing their breeches. (In truth, they sell them or gamble them away) and we are forced to replace the garments at once, because it is demoralizing to have males here in the naked state.

I know you understand that Father Trujillo and I can get along with little and, when there is nothing, can do what you and I have always done, i.e., "tighten our cords." But it is glaringly wrong for the King to send us out here to do a job and leave us without the necessities of life. Because we are priests dedicated to poverty because we are devoted to God and His work, the State assumes we can be ignored. "Let God take care of them," is the State's attitude. Fortunately He does.

Enough of all this wailing. I tell you these things not to add to your troubles but to give you pith for your report to the Father Guardian. We are converting the heathen, and that is the important thing.

Father Moreno sat for a time considering whether or not to ask Father Serra when he might be expected to be relieved, but decided the Father President had more pressing problems to think about. Moreover, Father Serra himself had been in the field for many years and apparently had never thought of retiring to the comparatively quiet life of the College. He resumed writing:

One of the great difficulties we have is in administering the sacraments. If only the Californians would refrain from adultery, I would have no qualms about admitting them to Holy Communion. As it is, I wonder if we are not announting them before they are acceptable.

Father Moreno closed the letter with *Believe me, Dear Father, to be your least Brother who loves you in Jesus Christ* and took it next door to Father Trujillo who was engaged in trying to shave his tonsure. "Perhaps you have something to add." He handed his fellow priest the letter and asked, "What are you trying to do?"

"I didn't want to bother you."

"Here—" Father Moreno took the razor and set about scraping the stubble.

When Father Trujillo had finished reading the report he said, "There is one thing: I wish you'd tell the Father President that, while I made the vows of a friar minor, since coming here I haven't been able to devote myself to my calling."

Father Moreno took a side-step to look at his companion's face. He was not jesting. "I am so busy digging clay, mixing lime, making bricks, administering to the sheep, cows and goats, driving carts, hauling stones and hewing timbers I don't have time for prayer or meditation."

"It's all God's work."

"When they sent me out here nobody told me I'd be digging more than I preach and pray."

Father Moreno laughed, finished the tonsure, blew away the whiskers and said, "There, you've been reconfirmed."

Father Trujillo got up and took the razor. "Now it's your turn." Father Moreno sat down on the stool. "Just think," the younger priest said, "in Mexico and Cadiz and Barcelona priests are preaching and praying and meditating." He tested the razor's edge, found it wanting and paused to strop it.

Father Moreno said, "You sound as if you regret entering the priesthood."

"No, no! Heavens no! I'm not sorry. But by and large, I have been rewarded. Entering the priesthood is like getting married, for better or for worse, and a man would be foolish to dwell on his wife's faults."

"Are you suggesting that the Church has faults?"

"Anything that's man-administered has faults." Because of the coarseness of the hair the razor made a loud scraping sound. "You know what our critics say?" Father Trujillo went on, "They say we who call ourselves men of God are but feeding our egos by denying ourselves the worldly life and that we have set ourselves apart for vanity's sake."

"Doubtless there is a modicum of truth in it," the older man said.

"A priest would be no good if he were sinless."

"Then I should be a very good friar indeed."

Father Moreno chuckled. "You boast, of course."

Father Trujillo was saying his office in his cell early one morning when Consuelo appeared at his door with her young child. The child was crying and Consuelo's chocolate cheeks, too, were wet with tears. The priest was not pleased to be thus interrupted and there was a certain sharpness in his voice when he greeted them.

"Look what El Loco did," she said pointing to a blister on the child's hand. "He put fire there."

The priest examined the wound. "You mean he deliberately burned her?"

Consuelo nodded, repeating the word burned awkwardly.

"What for?"

"She cry. He no like."

Father Trujillo looked out the door. Old Birdwing, the shaman, was sitting on the ground next to the *cocina*, asleep. "Tell El Loco I want to see him," the priest said.

"He no here now."

"Well tell him when he comes back."

Consuelo made no move to go. The way she was standing he could see down the neck of her shift. It irked him that he could not avert his eyes. "Tell El Loco I want to see him," he repeated uncomfortably. Consuelo reluctantly turned to go. She moved away, leading the child by a hand. The priest followed the movement of her buttocks and felt a pang of guilt. He wondered if Father Moreno were susceptible to such carnality. Other priests, particularly those in missionary posts far from the watchful eye of authority, were said to have taken to bed native women. Some priests apparently had no sexual drive. Unhappily he was not that way. But having taken the vow of chastity there was no relief. Even masterbation was wrong. Fortunately nature had a way of applying pressure that would not be denied. These discharges took place while one was asleep: there was no sin in them. But there was sin in his lusting for Consuelo.

The young priest knelt and confessed to God and asked his forgiveness.

Across the patio Ignacio watched Consuelo sashay down the cloister and thought to himself: "I've got to have me some of that," and felt no guilt whatever.

Toward evening El Loco appeared carrying a string of fish, one of them a garabaldi. He presented himself to Father Trujillo, who was in the *cocina* making altar-bread. "I bring Father fish," the Indian said, holding up his catch. "Fish goddam good."

The priest was appalled. "Who taught you to say that?"

"Say what?"

"Take God's name in vain!"

"Pepito, he tell me."

"Don't ever let me hear you say it again. It is a bad word. Bad, bad, *bad*!—do you understand?"

The young man nodded, cowed.

"God will be angry."

El Loco held out the fish as compensation for his blasphemy.

"Why did you burn your child?" the priest asked, his voice shrill with vexation. The Indian did not reply but continued to hold out the string of fish as a peace offering. Father Trujillo snatched the fish and flung them onto the table. They lay inert, their walleyes staring fixedly at the priest. "I'll teach you not to burn anyone again," Father Trujillo said, seizing a poker from the glowing coals. He caught the Indian by an arm and applied the red-hot poker to his chest. The astonished El Loco leaped like a frog and, shrieking, fled, leaving some of his flesh sizzling on the end of the poker. "That will teach you not to burn little children," the priest shouted after him, brandishing the poker.

The explosive scene attracted several onlookers, among them Pepito, and seeing him, Father Trujillo shouted. "You should be ashamed of yourself, Pepito!—Teaching El Loco to blaspheme!"

The boy was taken aback, "What do you mean, Father?"

"You taught him to take the Lord's name in vain."

"No, no, Father! It is not true. The soldiers were teasing him. It was a joke."

"Unless you change your ways you'll end up in the bottomless pit."

When Father Moreno returned from a proselytizing visit to a distant rancheria, El Loco met him at the gate and showed him the wound Father Trujillo had inflicted. The Father Superior found his younger brother in his quarters. "What in God's name have you done to El Loco, Salvatore?"

Father Trujillo stiffened. "He burned his child. I thought I should show him how it feels."

"But we must not hurt these people. It will undermine all we are trying to do. Our image must be love and kindness."

"But Father Serra himself prescribes the lash."

"The lash, yes. A hot poker, no."

"But what he did, Father, is unforgivable. A lash is not enough."

"Then do as we did in the Sierra Gordo. When a native committed a felony the garrison would seize him and condemn him to death. As he was about to be hanged I would appear and implore the soldiers for the sake of Jesus to spare his life. They would then resort to the lash. Once a few strokes had been laid on I would inform the wrongdoer that if he had learned his lesson God would forgive him. It worked like magic. Thereafter for the rest of his days he would give us no trouble."

"You mean you staged it like a play?"

"If you want to call it that."

"But is not that dishonest?"

"It does the trick. It garners souls. And that is why we are here. If El Loco leaves the Mission others may go with him and much of our work will have gone for naught."

The younger priest's slight figure appeared to slump. "But he burned a helpless child!"

Father Moreno turned to go. "I'd appreciate it," he said, "if you would go and apply some ointment to his wound. The only way we're going to take that cruelty out of him is through kindness."

Father Trujillo took a long moment to say, "At your orders, Father."

CHAPTER SEVEN

To celebrate the Mission's second birthday, Father President Serra returned to San Simeon to administer the Sacrament of Confirmation to those Indians who had been baptized. He was delighted with the Mission's progress and during his stay confirmed eighty-four neophytes. He brought with him a directive issued by the New Governor of Upper California, Filipe de Neve, calling for neophytes at each Mission to elect leaders from among their own ranks—two *alcaldes* and two *rigidores* or councilmen. These native officials were to have certain powers and were to be exempt from punishment.

"Apparently the Government wants to give the native Californians a taste of democracy," Father President told the resident priests. "Democracy seems to be very popular these days. The whole idea is patently absurd and I told the Governor it will not work. We tried it at San Carlos. A certain Baltazar was chosen one of the *alcaldes* and no sooner had he realized his privileges, especially in exemption from chastisement, than he did what he pleased. He seduced his sister-in-law and beat with a stick a neophyte. Because I demoted him he ran away, lives in concubinage, sends messages to the people here urging them to desert, and generally has caused us nothing but trouble. Nevertheless, the Governor says we must go on with this experiment. I suggest you appoint but one *alcalde* and let that suffice for the 'election.' I will then report to the Governor that you have complied."

Father Moreno appointed El Loco *alcalde*, or mayor, but told him nothing of any exemption from punishment. Thereafter it was his job to get the neophytes to Mass and to make them behave according to Christian precepts. As his badge of office, El Loco wore a hat of straw embellished with birdfeathers, and it was amusing to see how pridefully he accepted his responsibilities.

Before he departed Father Serra went over with Father Trujillo the plans for the great church the latter had designed. It was to be in the form of a cross and would contain a sanctuary, a transept, a baptistry, a vestry, and a belltower. "I want to build it of stone," the architect said, "so that it will endure for a thousand years. I want it to be a temple worthy of the Divine Majesty who will be worshipped therein. And I want it to surpass in beauty and spiritual quality every church in California. We have found sources of lime and cement. All we need is a master mason. I am hoping that in your travels you might find one for us."

Father Serra said he would do what he could, but he was not optimistic. "We could use a dozen such," he said. "In these parts they are a rare breed."

"I am eager to start the church because it will take a long time to build," Father Trujillo said, "and I want to see it finished before old age forces me to retire. Meanwhile we have plans to rebuilt the chapel. It is entirely inadequate, as you know. And the wheat is doing so well we have to build a granary."

"Well, don't get so immersed in secular work that you neglect spiritual affaris."

In taking his leave, Father Serra embraced first Father Trujillo and then Father Moreno. The two old friends stood, arms about each other, for several moments without speaking. When finally they parted Father Serra said, "I am sorry for your sake, Georgio, that you are still here, but I am glad for God's sake, because you are doing much wondrous work."

"Don't let the matter trouble you, Father. God seems to want me here and as long as He does, I am happy to do His will."

While the priests were occupied from sunup to sundown, day in and day out, making and laying bricks, planting and harvesting crops, proselytizing, teaching and administering to the sick, the soldiers had little to do. By Royal decree the garrison was under the jurisdiction of the priests to whom it was assigned, but there was no obligation on the part of the soldiers to do manual labor. However, Father Moreno managed to get a good deal of work out of them by flattery and the judicious granting of absolutions.

As the squad's leader, Ignacio particularly considered himself superior to travail. Thus it was unusual for him to appear bright and early one morning to lend a hand with the bricklaying. Father Moreno expressed his surprise jestingly: "What iniquity are you atoning today, Ignacio?"

53

Ignacio pretended to be aggrieved. "Why, Father Georgio, how you talk! I have come to help because it grieves me to see you and Father Salvatore working so hard."

The truth is: Ignacio had become enamored of a young girl who had recently come to the Mission. Christened Inez, she was, for a native Californian, an exceptionally attractive child. It seemed that all of the factors which had gone into her composition were in harmony and balance, and besides being beautiful she had a flair and a beguiling insouciance. Though only twelve she typically was well developed physically. As he went about his duties Ignacio composed speeches to her, to be delivered whenever he found the opportunity. They had a monotonous theme: "You are a fine vessel to hold a child and if you permit me I will supply you with same. I can furnish you a beautiful baby, one which will have good Spanish blood in him and one which may grow up to become a general or even a Pope. I will supply you this child free of charge; in fact, for the privilege I will give you my boots and a month's wages, providing I ever get paid. . ."

Sometimes in thinking of her his thoughts were loftier than that. Sometimes he thought just the caress of her hands might be sufficient to ease the pain in his groin and quench the fire in his mind. Sometimes his imagination even soared poetically and because of her he thought of the miraculousness of life and at other times he thought that if he could have intercourse with her he might even begin to believe in God.

Later that day, observing Ignacio looking lasciviously at Inez, Father Trujillo said to his superio: "I think, Father, it is time we built the *monjerio*."

To forestall extramarital intercourse and any resultant hostility on the part of the barbarian males, the *monjerio*, or apartment for unmarried girls, had become a part of the Mission plan. Here it was the custom to lock up at night, out of temptation's way, the unattached females. It was a naive approach to the persistent problem, and the sexual urge being what it is, never worked very well; but it did serve as a restraint.

Father Moreno paused, brick in hand, a splotch of mud on a cheek, to say, "Sooner or later we're going to have to." He placed the brick and slapped a dollop of mud on it. "The soldiers should marry these girls. That way they will spread the King's Spanish. I'm told there is no classroom to compare to the conjugal bed. Moreover, their offspring will be born in the Church."

"It seems that all of man's ills are due to the sexual urge."
"Likewise, obviously, his blessings."

It is early morning. The neophytes and soldiers are gathered in the ramshackle chapel for religious instruction. Father Trujillo is preaching. He has bared his chest and is beating it with a stone. So hard does he strike himself that blood appears. It seems likely he will crack his ribcage. The words of his sermon are trumpeted and high-pitched, calculatedly to put the fear of God in the congregation.

Father Moreno, seated at one side of the small dias, vaguely wishes his fellow priest would not be so effusive. To be sure, he had seen Father Serra beat himself that way, still to him there was a theatricalism about it which fanaticized the office. The motley gathering before him evokes a feeling of poignancy. It disturbs him that he feels depressed. Depression and doubt are devices of the Devil. He tries to shake off the feeling that the entire endeavor at the Mission is hopeless. Is it possible that these savages would ever become civilized? Is it possible they can ever learn to observe the Christian moral code? His gaze wanders over the assembled and stops on Ignacio's face. The soldier's attention is not on Father Trujillo but on Inez, and he is looking at her with such lickerishness that he appears idiotic. On the other hand, Inez, seated beside El Loco, is fascinated to the point of hypnosis by the preacher. As for El Loco, his reaction to the sermon is to slap his thighs in appreciation. Father Moreno closes his eyes for a moment of meditation.

Following the religious service, the congregation repaired to the patio for language instruction under the tutelage of Father Moreno and Pepito. This morning, to explain the Resurrection, Father Moreno resorted to an old trick invented by the Jesuit Father Kino: he put flies in water until they, to all appearances, were dead, then took them out and placed them in the sunshine. The warmth of the rays soon revived the insects and they flew away.

The natives were astonished by this performance. *"Puputepe! Puputepe!"* they exclaimed, thus furnishing Father Moreno with a Chumash word to explain the death, resurrection and ascension of Christ.

Pepito was more proficient in Chumash than Father Moreno, so he did most of the lay teaching. This morning he led the class to the corral and pointed to the bull. "You see this big cow," he said in

Chumash. "He is called a *toro*. He is full of little cows—*vacas*. We bring him with us because he preserves the little *vacas* until they are ready to be born. He is a marvelous fellow, this *toro*. He is called Christopher Colombo."

Later that morning, Ignacio drew Pepito aside and, with an affability never shown the child before, said, "How you feel, Pepito?" He put an arm about the boy's shoulders.

Pepito was pleased but curious. "Good," he said.

"I was listening to you teach those Indians," Ignacio said, leading the boy behind the guardhouse. "You are very smart."

"You hear them?" the boy asked pridefully. "They say the names of the Trinity today."

Ignacio nodded. "You are very good. I like to have you teach me Indian talk."

"Sure. I teach."

Ignacio looked askance to see that they were not being overheard and said, "How you like to shoot my gun, Pepito?"

The youth looked up quickly, eagerly. "Shoot gun?" he asked incredulously.

"Sure. I let you shoot."

The boy was delighted with the prospect, but there was in his demeanor a racial reserve and caution. "I never shoot gun before," he said.

Ignacio's manner was easy and confidential. He smiled toothfully at the youth's suppressed excitement and clapped him on the back. "What you want to kill?—You want to kill deer, maybe?"

"May I no can kill deer."

"You don't kill deer," Ignacio said, chuckling. "The gun does it for you. But don't tell the padres." The man frowned to impress the warning upon the boy. Pepito nodded. Ignacio went on, "What goes on between you and me—that's our business. We don't have to tell anybody. You're a good boy and I like you and that is why I am going to let you shoot my gun. You understand?"

"Yes."

"*Bueno*." Then Ignacio said, "There's just one little thing I'd like you to do for me—" and hesitated, watching the boys face for a reaction. Pepito raised his black eyebrows inquiringly. "You know how to talk Indian talk."

"I teach you."

"I know, but that'll take a while. I want to say something now. So

I want you to say it for me."

The boy shrugged. "Sure. I say."

"You know Inez—I want you to talk to her. I want you to tell her I want to see her. Point me out to her." Ignacio drew himself up straight. "Tell her I want to see her," the man leaned down to emphasize the word, " *alone*. Will you do that for me?"

"Yes. Sure."

"Now what did I say?"

"You say you want to see her alone."

"Don't forget. Tell her to follow me, to watch me after supper and to follow me. Understand?"

Pepito nodded uncertainly. "Tell her I've got something I want to give her—a present. And she should follow me after it gets dark."

"How she find you in the dark?"

"Well, *just before* it gets dark. Tell her to follow me after supper. Tell her I've got a present for her."

The boy nodded. From close by they heard Father Trujillo call, "Ignacio!"

"But don't let anybody hear you tell her," Ignacio said to Pepito quickly. "Wait till she's alone in the *pozolera*, then tell her." The man slapped the boy on the rump. "You do that and I'll let you shoot my gun."

As they came from behind the guardhouse they came upon Father Trujillo. Ignacio said, "Yes, Father?"

The priest looked at them suspiciously. "What have you been up to?"

The soldier laughed uncomfortably. "Nothing, Father."

"I want you to go hunting with me."

"Hunting?—Sure, Father. What are we going to hunt?"

"Beams. We're going to put a new roof on the chapel."

Ignacio was confused. He brushed the moustache from his mouth with the back of a hand. "But there are no trees in this country, Father. There is only the scrub oak, the cottonwood and the sycamore. The oak is too small, the cottonwood too weak, and the sycamore too crooked."

"Don't be so faithless, Ignacio. God will supply the beams. He will lead us to them."

Ignacio furrowed his brow and glanced at Pepito. "How long will it be?" he asked.

The priest shrugged. "That is up to God. Saddle some horses."

God led the priest and the soldier up one canyon and then another, taking them ever higher into the hills. They found trees along the creek bed and on the northern slopes, but, as Ignacio said, they were too short, too crooked or too fragile. Such thick-trunked oaks as they came across were squat and gnarled.

"One can build as long as he pleases," Father Trujillo said as they rode along, "but he can build only as wide as his beams. The beam is to a roof what moral character is to a man." The priest looked askance at his companion to see if he had gotten the message. Ignacio gave no indication. They rode a way without speaking, with nothing but the stomp of the horses' hooves, the chirping of birds, and the apathetic squealing of the saddle leather to break the engulfing silence. "You know what is moral character, don't you, Ignacio?"

"Sure, Father."

"What is it?"

"It's obeying the Ten Commandments."

"Quite right. And not giving in to temptation. You know, don't you, Ignacio, that lying, cheating and stealing only lead to unhappiness?"

"If you get caught," Ignacio said, joking.

"Why have you never married?"

"Me? Marry?" The soldier laughed briefly. "Not me, Father."

"You are very cynical, Ignacio."

"I never claimed to be a saint, Father," Ignacio said, and abruptly changed the subject. "You are an educated man, Father. What do you make of this life? What's it all about?"

Father Trujillo replied readily, as if he had answered the question many times: "There is no factual answer. No mathematical equation can explain it. God is the Great Intelligence which created the Universe and He is the only one who knows the answer. That is the reason you must have faith, faith in His guidance and wisdom. If you live up to His laws He will tell you the answer. For those who follow His precepts, the reward is everlasting life. For those who go their own sinful ways, there is only agony and frustration."

"Do you really believe that, Father?"

"Why, what do you mean, do I believe it? Of course I believe it. It's the gospel truth."

"I think about the meaning of life a lot," the soldier said, "and I never have been able to find any reasonable answers."

"That's because you don't have faith, faith in God."

58

"How do you go about getting faith, Father? Do you just quit asking questions?"

"Precisely. Put all doubt out of your mind. Accept the guidance of God. He will answer the questions for you."

Ignacio nodded, then shook his head. He was not convinced, but decided not to pursue the matter.

"It's as simple as that," the priest said as they rode on.

After a little while Ignacio said, "I'm afraid I'll never get to Heaven, Father. There's not a Commandment I haven't broken."

"It's never too late to repent." The missionary took off his wide-brimmed black hat and wiped his brow with a forefinger, flung off the moisture and then wiped the finger on his horse. "If you put temptation behind you," he went on, replacing the hat on his hand, "you will find that life can be beautiful."

The soldier did not comment.

"There's beauty all about us," the priest said. "What is the most beautiful thing you ever saw?"

"I'm sorry, Father, the prettiest thing I ever saw was a naked woman."

"What else?"

"Number seven on the dice." The soldier grinned to show he was joking.

"I'm afraid you're incorrigible, Ignacio."

"I guess maybe you're right, Father."

They rode on in silence for a while, then Father Trujillo asked, "Have you ever been in love, Ignacio?"

"No, Father, I don't believe I have."

"Maybe that's your problem."

"Were you ever in love, Father?"

"I was."

"With a woman?"

"Yes. I was thirteen. She was older than I. It broke my heart when she married. I don't think she was aware how deeply I loved her."

"Is that why you turned to the priesthood?"

"It could have been a factor. But I think I was born to be a priest."

"Is a priest really chosen by God to effect His will on earth?"

"We like to think so, but it really is individual desire. Some young men are attracted to religion just as some are attracted to the army."

"Why did you become a priest?"

59

"Well, for one thing, there were eleven children in my family and my mother wanted one of us to go into the Church. Then too, I was idealistic; I wanted to help man, to save him from sin."

"That's a large order. Sometimes I think you are disappointed."

"I'm not as zealous as I once was," the priest said. "I've learned as one grows older that his ambition declines."

"You mean you don't want to be the Pope?"

Father Trujillo made a wry face. "There is not a chance." he said.

Ignacio rode on a bit before saying, "I could never have become a priest. Religion never interested me."

"It's very important—more so than anything. Without religion, Ignacio, man would be like the apes. There would be no education, no peace, no love, and there would be nothing but wickedness in the world."

Ignacio grinned. "For all your effort, that's about the way it is right now."

Father Trujillo said nothing and they rode on in silence.

Toward mid-afternoon of the second day they came into a high valley wherein grew a goodly number of pine and cedar trees of sufficient height and thickness to beam the chapel. Father Trujillo chose sixteen of the tallest ones—one for each Commandment and precept of the Church—and marked them. The length of all the beams, seventeen feet, was determined by the shortest trunk the thickness by the thinnest.

"God has supplied the beams," the priest said, as they started back, "now all we need is a second miracle to get them down the mountainside."

Father Moreno suggested that getting the logs to the Mission be made a contest and by doing so managed to enthuse the natives into participating. Two teams, each with twenty of the strongest males, were chosen for the competition. Ten of each team would carry a log, racing for half a mile; it would then be picked up by their teammates. Alternating in this way, laughing and joking as they came, the Indians carried the logs down the mountainside. The team which delivered eight logs to the Mission in the least time received a cow, the losers, two goats. However it was not the prizes so much that motivated the bearers as it was the contest itself. The round trip covered about forty miles, and it required but eight days to complete the job. Not half an hour separated the winners from the losers.

Californians are exceedingly good runners. Father Moreno wrote in his journal. *I grow much more weary in the saddle than they do walking. They will jog for many hours without showing fatigue. Some years ago when he was eight or nine years old Pepito offered to accompany me on a journey, but I told him that my horse was speedy and he could not keep up. "Your horse will tire,"* he replied, *"but I will not."*

CHAPTER EIGHT

As the last words of the benediction were intoned in the evening air, Ignacio, who hadn't been paying much attention to the religious proceedings, set out across the patio headed for the rear gate, there where the stockade joined the corral. Here he stopped and waited. He could see the group milling about outside the chapel and beyond it the little hill-hunched valley and the sea. The setting sun, diffused by a screen of clabber clouds, was a brilliant orange. A stillness was on the land as if the world had paused.

Ignacio waited impatiently for what seemed to him a long time and, when Inez failed to detach herself from the group, began to doubt that Pepito had given her his message. Two horses thrust their oblong heads over the corral fence and stared at him in that ear-raised, dumb way of horses. Startled, the soldier flung an arm toward them saying, "*Vayan!*" irritatedly. The horses jerked up their heads but otherwise did not move. They continued to regard the man with big, chestnut eyes. "Go on," Ignacio said, and took a threatening step. When neither horse moved he muttered, "God-dam horses!" and made a mental note not to confess the sin. Then, inasmuch as he was not going to confess it, he repeated the oath. Picking up a stone he threw it over the horses, whereupon both turned and trotted away.

Concluding that Inez was not coming, Ignacio started to retrace his steps, but as he did so he saw her pick up a basket and start toward him, moving with a nice rhythm down the path between the young fruit trees and the vegetable garden. Elated, he returned to the gate and stood there to make sure she saw him, then, tossing his head as an indication she should follow him, went on down the path toward the creek. At the foot of the incline he waited for her to appear before leaving the path and pushing through clumps of waist-high mustard, moving upstream. Inez hesitated in the gateway, her slender body framed against the color-rich sky, then sashayed on down the path swinging the basket. Ignacio watched as she approached the place he had left the path. She did not give any indication she had seen him, and for a moment it appeared she would go on toward the spring; but then, a few steps beyond where he had turned off, she paused to look back and darted quickly into the mustard, crouching as she ran. Ignacio caught her hand and pulled her down so clumsily that she fell into his arms. "*Dispense me,*" he whispered. Hunger born of a long fast was in him. It surprised him somewhat that she made no resistance to his advances. The skin of her breasts was smooth and taut and the nipples hardened almost at once. When in his frenzy he hurt her, her howl had a bitter sound like that of a coyote. "Shhh!" he hissed.

She squeezed the hurt out of her wounded breast and said something uncomplimentary in Chumash. Now when he resumed his lovemaking she was not so compliant. He persisted, however, and gradually she responded. The sudden oncoming sound of hurrying footsteps and Father Trujillo's voice: "Inez!" caused the lovers to freeze. Ignacio put a hand over Inez's mouth.

"You Ignacio!—Inez!—" They could hear the priest pushing through the high mustard. "I know you're in there," he said, pressing forward and peering into the weeds.

Discovery being inevitable, Ignacio got to his feet smiling disarmingly. "Good evening, Father."

Father Trujillo stopped. "There you are! Where's Inez?"

"Inez?" Ignacio asked with false innocence.

"Don't you lie to me, Ignacio. I saw her come down here."

"She must have gone on to the spring."

"The spring indeed!" the priest said, and pressed forward to see for himself. Whereupon Ignacio, laughing, said, "I was only joking, Father," and helped the girl to her feet. "We were taking a little siesta."

"I know what you were doing," Father Trujillo said, looking at Inez, who had covered her face with her hands. "I don't wonder you're ashamed," he said to her.

Ignacio said, "We haven't done anything wrong," self-righteously.

The priest took the girl's hand and, pulling her, started back up the incline toward the Mission. Ignacio, undecided what to do, followed. Father Trujillo went to the storehouse where Father Moreno was checking the supplies by candlelight. "You told me you wanted to approve the punishments," the younger priest said. "Well, I have brought you two culprits. I caught them in *flagrante delicto.*"

63

Father Moreno held the candle so that its rays fell on the three faces. "What have you been up to, Ignacio?"

Father Trujillo said, "They were lying together in the grass. We must make an example of him, Father."

Father Moreno sat down wearily on a sack of grain. It had been a long day. The burden of his office never weighed so heavily as when he had to pronounce judgement. For teaching he felt he had some talent, but he had often admitted to himself that he was a poor judge. It seemed to him that the gravity of a crime depended on what was in the perpetrator's heart at the time it was committed. Considering that no man is blameless, how could one man judge another? "How many times have I told you, Ignacio?" he asked.

"I met Inez on the way to the spring, Father. We sat down together. I was trying to teach her some Spanish words."

Father Trujillo: "They were lying in the grass."

"You like this girl?" Father Moreno asked the soldier.

"She is all right."

"Would you be willing to marry her?"

"Now Father," Ignacio said, "you know I'm not the marrying kind." He did not want to say in Inez's presence that he considered Californians too inferior to take to wife; all right for lovemaking, but not suitable for marriage.

"God would be pleased."

"I'm sorry, Father."

Father Moreno thought how important to the Mission was this dissident soldier. While he sometimes seemed to be a tool of the Devil he had many good qualities, not the least of which were cleverness, candor and common sense. The Father Superior spoke to Father Trujillo: "Did you catch them in the act, Salvatore?"

"Well, not exactly. But why else would they be hiding in the grass?"

"If you didn't catch them in the act the evidence is circumstantial. We can hardly convict on that."

"We've already been too lenient with him, Father. I think he should be reported to his superior."

Father Moreno said, "That way we lose him. Who would command the garrison?"

"They would send a replacement."

"There is no assurance his replacement's morals would be any better. Anyway, it would be hard to replace Ignacio. He is good at his job. Would you consider giving him another chance?"

Father Trujillo's disappointment was evident. As a prosecutor he thought he had an open-and-shut case. "Well," he said reluctantly, "if he gives us his word of honor he'll leave the girls alone?"

Father Moreno said, "See that you leave the girls alone, Ignacio."

"Yes, Father." As Ignacio turned to go, Father Trujillo said, "I don't suppose the girl understands that she has done anything wrong."

"Probably not."

Father Trujillo spoke to Inez in broken Chumash: "Do you realize that you have committed a sin?"

"What is a sin, Father?"

"A sin is a violation of God's law." The priest could tell by the girl's expression that she still did not understand. He was going to have to be more specific. "God's law says you are not to cohabit until you are married. If you can get one of the soldiers to marry you God would be pleased."

Father Moreno said, "Use your feminine charms to good effect."

"What I do?" the girl asked.

"Keep your legs crossed," Father Moreno said, a statement so startling it ended the interview.

The quiet of a Sunday afternoon was shattered by the sound of a gunshot. Both priests emerged from their cells. Indians and dogs, sleeping in the shady side of the patio, likewise were aroused. From a distance came a thin cry. The priests, followed by Indians and dogs, hurried toward the rivergate. When they reached it they saw Pepito coming up the slope. He was crying.

"What's the matter, boy?" Father Moreno cried, advancing toward him. "Are you hurt?"

Pepito shook his head, turned and pointed to Ignacio, on his knees near the riverbed. "Ignacio, he let me shoot his gun. It go off, quick."

"You shot Ignacio?"

The boy nodded, sobbing, "I no mean to."

When Father Moreno reached him Ignacio was holding his right side just above the hip. His tunic was bloody and blood was on his hands. His normally swarthy face was ashen. He took his hands from the wound to reveal to the priests the cause of his prostration and in an anguished way was pleased that the evidence was so convincing. "I

65

was showing the boy the gun," he graoned. "It went off accidently."

"I did not mean to do it," Pepito said, sniffling.

"It was an accident," Ignacio said.

Father Trujillo said, "You mean to say you let that boy have your gun?" accusingly. Father Moreno put a hand on the soldier's forehead. It was cold. Ignacio looked at him questioningly. Father Moreno squatted down to examine the wound. Father Trujillo slapped a mongrel which was trying to lick the wounded man's face, saying "Get out of here!" irritatedly. Father Moreno ripped Ignacio's shirt and used a piece of it to wipe off the blood.

"Is it bad, Father?" Ignacio asked. "Am I going to die?"

"Can you walk?"

"I don't know."

"Let's try." The priests helped the soldier to his feet and, supporting him between them, managed to get him up the slope and into his bunk. Father Trujillo went off to boil some water.

"If God gives me another chance, Father," Ignacio said, "I promise I won't give Him any more trouble."

The priest recalled that several times in his life, under similar circumstances, he had heard such vows; and it was a discouraging truth that, once the pledgors were well and strong again, they forgot the obligation. Father Moreno thought it was as man is with money: in want he is inclined to be generous and abject; rich, stingy and imperious. "Mind what you say," he cautioned Ignacio. "Etch it indelibly."

"If I die, Father do you think Saint Peter will let me in?"

"He will if you confess your sins."

"Confess me now, Father." And Ignacio, who until then hadn't had much faith in anything except himself, repeated after the priest: "I confess to Almighty God, to blessed Mary ever Virgin, to blessed John the Baptist, to the holy Apostles Peter and Paul, and to all the Saints that I have sinned exceedingly in thought, word and deed, through my fault, through my fault, through my grievous fault. Therefore I beseech Mary, ever Virgin, blessed Michael and Archangel, blessed John the Baptist, the holy Apostles Peter and Paul, and all the Saints to pray to the Lord our God for me. May the Almighty and merciful Lord grant me pardon, absolution and remission of all my sins. Amen." Father Moreno then had the soldier repeat the Acts of Faith, Hope and Charity, which the latter should have known by heart but didn't, after which Ignacio lay back exhausted.

"Thank you, Father."

Father Moreno proceeded with his priestly duty. "All of us have to die some time," he said. "But what we call death, Ignacio, is but another phase of what we call life. They are parts of the same thing, like night and day." He spoke slowly to let the reassurance sink in. "One's body dies, but not the self, the soul. The soul never dies. Nothing," the priest went on, leaning forward on the three-legged stool, "is lost to the world, neither smoke, nor steam nor scent. Thus no one ever comes to a finality."

The single candle wreathing priest and patient revealed the hide bed and the clay chamberpot on the earthen floor. From outside came the voices of the soldiers discussing the accident. Jose was saying, "I was shot once—in the foot. The gun went off while I was loading it."

Father Moreno went on: "I believe it was through death that man first came to realize the existence of God. As a man approached death it was only natural that he came to wonder about the meaning of life. And he must have come to the realization that life isn't spontaneous and haphazard, because everything else is too orderly, methodical and harmonious—the seasons, time, the sun, moon and stars. He must then have asked himself, If there is a plan, what is it, and how do I fit into it? Each of us has his place. We're all important in the scheme, even the lowliest. And we must all have faith that this is so. You might ask, how can one believe in something when there is no evidence? That is what having faith means."

Father Trujillo brought the hot water and Father Moreno proceeded to wash the soldier's wound. Apparently the bullet had gone in the midriff and out the back. As yet there was no way to determine whether or not it had punctured a vital organ, but when the bleeding stopped Father Moreno was encouraged. Emerging from the guardhouse he told the other soldiers; "I think he is going to survive," and suggested they take their conversation elsewhere to give the patient a chance to sleep. He then crossed to the *cocina*, told Suegra to see to it Ignacio had food and water, and went to his cell. His talk with the wounded soldier for some reason had depressed him. He spent some time in prayer.

Later, toward evening, when he went out to relieve himself, he stood behind the fence looking at the darkening hills, at the tule-lined riverbed and at the outstretching sea. The evening star hung over the western horizon. Indians considered stars the hearts of chieftains and shamans who had departed this life, and it struck Father Moreno that this was a prime example of their abysmal ignorance. Then it occured to him that he himself was not certain what the stars were. The Bible says that the Lord created them, along with the sun and moon, to give light upon the earth, and of course there was no gainsaying the Bible. As a student, Father Moreno had read the profane Galileo's theory that the earth was a heavenly body which moved around the sun, but he had scorned it because it had been drilled into him that God had made the earth the center of the Universe. Now he wondered whether Galileo might not have been right, as some scientists averred. If he was right, the Bible was in error, and if the Bible was in error in one part who could rely upon it for trust in another?

Father Moreno tried quickly to snuff out such blasphemous thoughts, attributing them to the Devil's cunning. But some of them kept recurring, and one persistent question which had plagued him ever since he had been observing mankind in his primitive state was: Had God created man in His image, or was it the reverse? Another was: If God is all-powerful and all-knowing, why does he visit so much misery on those who love and are faithful to Him? It often seemed to the priest that the heathen were happier on the earth than the devout. The only way this made sense was if one accepts the theory that God is testing and preparing the faithful for the Glorious Hereafter.

He looked upward at the blackening sky. "Oh, God, renew my faith. Do not permit me to stray from the path of righteousness." A deep, dolorous loneliness descended upon him, a feeling of abjection and melancholy. Gloaming had always been a time of sadness for him and, although he knew that with the coming of light his feeling of depression would diminish, he could not shake the feeling of futility. Darkness closed about him and still he stood, not hearing the cricket chorus nor feeling the quickening chill. "Do not brood over your fate," his mother had warned him, "or the eggs of hopelessness will hatch." It was a time to heed her. He returned to his cell, lit a candle and began to write of the matters which troubled him:

I sometimes wonder at my decision to come into this wilderness, to exchange a safe life and all I hold dear for hardship, loneliness and a thousand dangers. It is all but incredible that a man, even a priest, would leave his family and friends to consort with wild and inhuman savages to help them win the Kingdom of Heaven. There are times, as now, when I think that God could not possibly care what happens to these people. They do not appreciate what we are trying to do for them but return our kindnesses by thieving. Nothing to them is so important as a full stomach, and the fact that mine may be empty in no wise concerns them. They are a people without honor, shame or law. Today I delivered a sermon in praise of the Saints, explaining how they crushed all vanity, distributed their belongings among the poor, and subjected themselves to the most severe penances. I pointed out that the Saints slept on the ground, ate no meat, drank no wine; and after the service one of the Indians said to me that he always slept on the ground, that he had never tasted bread in his life, and that the only meat he had known was that of rats and mice, besides which he did not even know what wine was. And he wanted to know if that made him a Saint. Hallelujah!

CHAPTER NINE

Ignacio recovered steadily. The leaden bullet had passed through the flesh without puncturing either an artery or a vital organ, and miraculously no infection developed. Consuelo or Suegra visited the patient several times a day, administering to his needs.

One evening while Father Moreno was reading aloud from the Bible to Pepito, who unbeknownst to the priest had fallen asleep, there came from the patio gutteral words and scuffling and a woman's cry. Father Moreno closed the book on a finger to mark the place and, still carrying it, hurried outside. Dimly in the darkness he made out the struggling couple. "Here! Here!" he admonished them. "What's going on?" Even as he spoke the man struck the woman and she fell backward against the chapel. Her assailant kicked her. Father Moreno caught the man's arm. "Loco!" he cried. "What are you doing?"

"She is bitch dog," El Loco said.

"Shame on you!" The priest pushed the angry man to one side and helped Consuelo to her feet.

"She foul nest," El Loco said, and spat out of a side of his mouth to show disgust.

The woman spat back at him.

"I catch her with soldier," El Loco said.

"I take food to him like you say," Consuelo said to the priest.

El Loco said, "She no good. I am through with her."

Father Moreno spoke to Consuelo: "Tonight you stay in the monjerio," and to Loco: "Lay a hand on her again, Loco, and it will be the lash. Understand?"

The Indian turned away without replying and went off into the darkness.

For several days thereafter El Loco was absent from the Mission. Rumor filtered through that he was in a distant *rancheria* holding mock religious services and preaching. José and Vincenti were assigned to bring him back, but just as they were getting under way he

70

reappeared. Now there was in him none of the gay spirit, the zaniness, humor and bouyancy which had been such strong attributes of his personality. He went about his duties morosely, taking little interest in either the Mission or those within it. He even quit wearing his badge-of-office cap. Father Moreno made a strong effort to renew their compatible relationship, but to little avail. "His ego has been wounded," he told Father Trujillo, "and I'm afraid it will be some time before he recovers. It is characteristic of these people that they never forget an affront."

Idle hands and sin were synonymous to Father Trujillo and it was inevitable that he and El Loco would come to a confrontation. The encounter occured while Father Moreno was away. The younger priest was engaged in tiling the roof of the chapel. His supply of mortar having run out, he called to his helpers to bring more. Getting no response, he descended the ladder and came upon Jiminez, Rudolpho and Felipe playing *tousee* with El Loco. The game was played with two on a side, the players squatting opposite one another. While one player, with elaborate gestures, tries to distract the opposing team, his partner hides a pebble in a hand behind his back. The most profound silence then ensues while the adversaries study the face of the holder, trying to ascertain in which hand the stone is held. "Jiminiz!" Father Trujillo cried. "Rudolpho!—" The Indians, at a climactic point in the game, pretended not to hear him. But when he called to them a second time, all save El Loco skurried away. Without moving from his squatting position, El Loco looked up defiantly at the oncoming priest.

"You're not content with being a lazy, good-for-nothing lout yourself," Father Trujillo said, standing over him; "you've got to corrupt the others!" El Loco did not reply. The priest went on: "What you need is a good whipping."

The Indian uttered one word, which the priest did not understand.

"What did you say?"

El Loco gazed silently at the priest without expression.

"Don't you curse me!" Father Trujillo exclaimed, picking up a reed. But before he could apply it, the Indian sprang up, snatched the switch from him, broke it in two, then with an air of regal disdain walked across the patio and out the main gate.

His wickiup was still burning when Father Moreno returned and as the two priests stood watching the glowing, crackling embers, ("Fleas giving up the ghost," Father Moreno said.) Father Trujillo recounted what had transpired.

"I assume he has gone," the younger priest concluded. "And if you ask me, it's good riddance."

"No matter what either of us thinks of him," Father Moreno said, "he has much influence. We shall have to bring him back."

"But, Georgio, he has not one single virtue. He is selfish, avaricious, covetous and, I have no doubt, murderous."

Father Moreno extended an arm in extravagant gesture to include the hills and the sea. "Behold!—a republic of Hell inhabited by a diabolical union of apostates!" And, as they turned toward the Mission gate, he went on: "It is true: Californians are the most pitiable of all Adam's children, and yet I sometimes wonder if they are not better off than we are. We came out here to enlighten them, and I'm beginning to wonder if we are doing the right thing."

Father Trujillo was too shocked to comment.

"So far as this world is concerned," Father Moreno went on, "these people seem to be far happier than our brothers and sisters in Europe. They are free of the concerns which plague civilized men and women. With Californians there is no mine and thine, two words which, as Saint Gregory says, fill the days of our lives with untold bitterness and evil."

"They have nothing."

"And yet at all times they have whatever they need and as much as they need of it. Note that they are always in high spirits and that they laugh and joke continually. It seems that God does not love them any the less for their ignorance."

They approached the main gate. Ignacio was standing in the guardhouse doorway. Falco was sitting on a stool plunking a guitar and singing:

"Fly not yet, 'tis just the hour
When pleasure, like the midnight flower
That scorns the eye of vulgar light
Begins to bloom for sons of night
And maids who love the moon. . ."

Father Moreno paused to ask Ignacio how he was feeling.
"Tolerable, Thank you, Father."
"I trust you appreciate God's help?"
"Oh, yes, Father. I am very grateful."
"Remember your vow."

"What's that, Father?"

"You mean you've forgotten already? You vowed that if God would spare your life you would never give Him cause to punish you again. Remember?"

"Oh, that?—Yes, Father. I am a new man and I thank our Heavenly Father for it."

"In that case, your experience may have been worth it," And Father Moreno thought: *God can come from evil as a flower can grow from a mound of manure.* "It looks," he said, "as if El Loco has left us."

"I see he burned his house."

"The pitahayas are getting ripe and it may be he has gone to gorge himself, but I fear otherwise. He has probably gone to the hot springs. I am going to see if I can persuade him to come back. Falco I want you to come with me."

Of all the foods available to the Californians, the fruit of the pitahaya cactus Father Moreno referred to was by far their favorite. It is red and spiney and has a high sugar content. In California, pitahayas begin ripening in late June and last through August. For the natives that was carnival time. Indeed, they gauged the year from one pitahaya season to the next. It was nothing for a Californian to eat twenty-five pounds of pitahayas in one day. The effect was a happy drunkenness. The fruit contains many seeds which, for some reason, are not digested in the human stomach. The natives would collect these from excrement and would roast, grind and, with much joking, eat them. They called the second harvest.

Californians will eat almost anything that teeth can masticate, Father Moreno wrote in his journal. *Roots and seeds of all kinds and the flesh of any living thing: birds, dogs, cats, horses, asses, mules, lice, rats, snakes, lizards, bats and owls, grasshoppers, crickets, caterpillars and worms. They even eat the bones of poultry, sheep and goats and the hides of cattle. In one village I came upon an old blind man who was pounding on a worn out deerskin shoe and stuffing the softened pieces into his toothless jaws. . .*

When a Californian died it was the custom for his or her relatives and friends to assemble for a *fiesta.* Such wakes were always at the instigation of a shaman whose power to a great extent derived from his ability to communicate with the dead. Thus when El Loco got back to the hot springs and found that an old woman was about to be buried because she was no longer able to forage for herself, he decided to vary this custom by having a party for her before she died so that she could participate. He believed he had learned enough mumbo-jumbo from the priests to become a *hechicero* and he wanted to impress his peers with his new-found powers. Accordingly he announced to the old woman's relatives that he was going to get into communication with her husband, long since departed this life, and instructed them to bring food to appease the spirits which guarded the gate to the other world. Those who came to the funeral ceremony not only brought food but appropriately painted their bodies with carbon black and yellow clay to frighten off the evil spirits.

The women arranged themselves in a circle around the men. El Loco sat in the center with the old woman who, though very much alive, was about to be buried. He had provided himself with a stick from one end of which hung strands of human hair. He told his audience that the hair was from the head of the old woman's late husband and that presently he would have a conversation with him to find out how it was in the hereafter. First, though, he said, he would have to retire to commune with the good spirits, give them some food and persuade them to open the door. And taking the food with him, he retired to a wickiup.

When he emerged, belly full, El Loco resumed his place beside the old woman. Waving the haired stick he uttered some inarticulate sounds, blew a whistle, pretended to jerk himself into a trance, and announced that the old woman's deceased husband was now among them. Cries of amazement arose from the assembled. Women pulled at their hair and men made grotesque faces. After more mumbling and twitching, El Loco spoke: "How is it there where you are?"

Deceased: (Also spoken by El Loco, but in a falsetto voice). "Good. Here we have much water and many fruits."

El Loco: "You have many pitahayas?"

Deceased: "Many, many pitahayas. And the fishing is fine."

El Loco: "Are there any clever people there?"

Deceased: "None as clever as you."

El Loco: "Is there anyone else here that you can talk to?"

Deceased: "No one. Only you. You are the only one with the power."

El Loco: "Have you a place for you wife?"

Deceased: "I have a fine place. She will be happy here."

El Loco: "What advice have you for the people here?"

Deceased: "I advise everyone to heed you. You are the greatest. If they listen to you they will come to this place and be happy. Otherwise they will sink into the ocean and be eaten by sharks."

At this juncture El Loco got up and began to dance and chant, whereupon the wailing and weeping resumed. His song was a lugubrious dirge with startling shouts; and his dance was a series of ungraceful jumps, hops and gesticulations. Meanwhile several women, using wooden spades, began digging a grave nearby.

It was at this juncture that Father Moreno and Falco came trudging up out of the riverbed. The dancing and digging ceased. El Loco said, "Good afternoon, Father."

Father Moreno's face wore a stern expression. He said, "El Loco, you have burned your house and left the Mission without permission. Why?"

"The house was alive with fleas, Father, and the pitahayas are ripening."

"Who is to do your *alcalde* duties?"

El Loco raised his hands and shrugged, as if to say, "*Quien sabe?*" but he did not reply.

"I want you to come back to the Mission," the priest said. "You have a responsibility there."

"I cannot come now, Father, I am occupied. We are going to bury this old woman who is about to die."

Father Moreno turned his attention to the old woman, who, save that she was inordinately skinny, appeared to be in good health. "Are you not well?" the priest asked her.

For reply she smirked, showing her toothless gums, and shook her head. The priest felt her pulse. It was strong. "I am hungry," she said.

"She wants to eat all the time," El Loco said, "but she cannot forage and there is no one to do it for her."

"That is no reason to kill her," Father Moreno said. "Where is your charity?" But then he realized the question was idle because Californians did not know the meaning of the word and in their savage culture there was no disposition to benevolence.

El Loco said, "She has become a burden. Anyway, she has lived long enough."

"It is not so bad to die," the old woman said. "It is part of life."

"We are going to put her out of her misery," one of the other Indians said.

Father Moreno said, "You are going to do nothing of the kind. She's going back to the Mission with us. We will fatten her up. The pitahayas are ripening. There is enough food for everyone."

"She is too weak to walk," El Loco said.

"Then we will carry her." Father Moreno spoke sharply to the women: "Get her some food to give her strength," and several skurried to obey.

While the old woman ate, Father Moreno and a reluctant El Loco fashioned a litter of poles and matting. And when she had consumed every morsel brought her, they lifted the old woman into the conveyance and, with the priest and Falco in the rear and El Loco and a man named Tomaso in front, they set out for the Mission, the old woman letting wind at intervals all along the way.

In recording the incident, Father Moreno wrote:

Californians have no respect for their elders and are wont to burn or bury alive the helpless and handicapped to be rid of them. We have named the old woman Lolita. She realizes we have saved her life and is appropriately grateful. When she has regained her strength she would be ready for conversion. And I am sure, with the proper care, she has many more useful years to live. . .

CHAPTER TEN

From time to time it became necessary to send someone to the port of San Diego to post and pick up mail, to collect the garrison's pay, and to bring back supplies. This task as a rule fell to Ignacio, principally because, as Father Moreno said, "He's the only one we can trust." Thus when he became well enough to make the journey, Ignacio was dispatched.

"Whatever I've got coming in back pay," Jose said, as the envoy was preparing to leave, "bring me that much aguardiente."

"That goes for me, too," Vincenti said.

"And for the love of God," Pedro said, "bring us a new deck of cards. We can't read the spots on these old ones."

Ignacio chided the fat one: "Perhaps instead," he said, "I should bring you a pair of spectacles."

Father Trujillo said, "I remind you again to use your persuasive tongue to wheedle some ecclestical garments out of the padres at the Mission. You can truthfully tell them that we are in rags."

The brown skin tight around his smiling, gold-flecked eyes, Ignacio said: "I may never come back. I'll get the back pay and take ship for Mexico."

"You do," Falco said, "and God and I will hound you to the end of the earth."

Ignacio mounted, said, "Remember me kindly," and heeled his horse. The beast set out slowly, reluctantly, as if knowing a long journey lay ahead. Two mules loaded with animal skins followed on a tether. The skins would be traded for whatever they would bring.

The Mission group stood in silence watching the soldier and his beasts go down the slope ahead of their dust and disappear into the tules.

Father Moreno got up from his bunk and stood in the doorway

77

looking out blinkingly at the Indians sleeping in the shade of the half-roofed chapel and thought how unreasonable it is to ask a man to work after the mid-day meal. He then consulted the sundial, a slab of rock set in the head of a stump. It was, more or less, fifteen minutes to three o'clock. Father Trujillo trudged across the patio struggling under the weight of two buckets full of sloshing water, engaged in the seemingly endless task of making tiles.

Father Moreno followed him and said, "You work like a man trying to get rich."

"God's work must be done."

"Don't you ever take a siesta?"

"Sleep is for the night."

The younger priest added water to red clay and proceeded to trample the mud with his bare feet, kneading it to the proper consistency. "When you are out here working I cannot rest," Father Moreno said, a twinkle in his eye. "You make me feel guilty." He then removed his sandals and joined him.

"I am trying to atone for my sins," Father Trujillo said, the sweat rolling down his face and neck into the coarse fabric of his habit. The air was very still, almost oppressively so. Not a leaf was stirring, not a whiskered wheathead. Father Trujillo's body odor was strong and Father Moreno held his breath to avoid it. He thought: *Our odors, like our faults, are not evident to ourselves.* "I'll go get more water," he said.

As he turned away the earth lurched. The bell tinkled and the chapel itself seemed to sway as if reflected in a wavy pool. The dozing natives scrambled frantically to their feet and raced screaming to the center of the quadrangle, huddled there, drawn together against the might of the unseen. Only Birdwing remained where he was. "What are you afraid of?" he called to his companions. "If death is going to get you, he can reach you there, too."

Another shudder of the earth was followed by a series of sharp, cracking sounds like those of gunshot, and the corner of the chapel nearest Birdwing split open. Before the adobe fragment reached the ground the old shaman was through the main gate.

"Earthquake!" Father Moreno said almost inaudibly. Father Trujillo made the sign of the cross. Both priests stood without moving, waiting apprehensively. The earth did not perceptibly move again, but after a few seconds a stack of unset adobe bricks toppled over as if pushed by an unseen hand. After what seemed a long time, there being no more tremors, Father Moreno said, "I guess that's all," and he and Father Trujillo went over to examine the damage. As they were doing so, one of the Indians called out: "God house not strong."

The younger priest was quick to counter such blasphemy: "God's house is very strong. Nothing can shake it down."

"The roof, maybe he fall."

Father Trujillo went and stood in the chapel doorway. "There is nothing to be afraid of," he said, and pushed against the wall. "God's house is stronger than a mountain."

And Father Moreno raised his voice to say: "God has shaken us to remind us of our sins, not the least of which is laziness. You will do well to heed what he is telling you."

Father Moreno's journal: *Californians do not know the meaning of love and have no word for it. They respond to affection like animals, that is, if it is accompanied by food or something else of value. Our task is to teach them the meaning of love and the best way to do that is through the institution of marriage. As it is now, a boy and a girl will pair up as soon or shortly after they attain puberty. As a rule the female is the aggressor. When her sexual hunger reaches a certain intensity, she will seek a partner. Males generally enter the relationship because they want a servant they can command. Females tend to cater to their mates because the males are physically stronger and can abuse them. The Chumash word for husband means a man who abuses a woman. Wives are expected to be faithful in a sexual sense to their husbands, but it is not unusual for both wives and husbands to wander in different directions for several days in the incessant search for food, sleeping wherever and with whomever strike their fancies. Husbands tolerate this. "Out of sight, out of mind," is their attitude. But if a wife is deliberately unfaithful to her husband or leaves him for another man he may kill her. Children stay with their mothers until they are able to forage for themselves, then strike out on their own. . .*

The missionaries preached that marriage in the Church, besides being mandatory to enter the Kingdom of Heaven, meant mutual respect, sexual fidelity, cleaving one to the other and sharing food. And they decreed that a girl could not marry until she was twelve years old, a boy, fifteen.

It is one thing to make rules and quite another to enforce them, particularly when the rules go against the forces of nature. The *monjerio* was the most effective control the priests had. Its administration became the responsibility of Father Trujillo, Father Moreno telling him: "You are more qualified than I to be nature's policeman." Come gloaming then and the shades of night, the younger priest would see that Suegra rounded up her charges, shooed them into the nunnery and bolted the door, thus shutting out the Devil and his bag of temptations.

Of the *monjerio's* inmates, Inez was the prettiest and the most temptatious. At age twelve she was coming into womanhood, but she still preferred Pepito's attentions to those of the lustful soldiers. One day she and Pepito were shucking corn together in the storehouse when he, seized by an overwhelming impulse, caught her suddenly in his arms and awkwardly, roughly kissed her, the while half expecting her to resist him. Instead, she only leaned away from him a little, surprised but not displeased. So he kissed her again and, growing bolder, put a hand inside the neck of her dress. Inez shrank from his rough touch and pressed the breast into herself for relief from the strange, intoxicating pain. "Don't," she said. And she resisted him when he tried to lift her skirt. "Someone will come," she whispered, watching the doorway.

"No they won't."

Both started when a chicken, backlighted by the late-afternoon sunlight, suddenly appeared in the doorway.

"Yes they will."

"No they won't. I promise," he insisted. "We can hear them."

"I'm afraid."

"I won't hurt you," he whispered impatiently. "Just let me see."

"What for?"

The matter-of-factness of the question irked him. "Because—" he pleaded. "Please!"

"The padre will punish us."

"No he won't."

"Yes he will."

"They're both in the field. I saw them go."

"Somebody else will come."

"Please, Inez—"

She permitted him to push her hands up a little, then a little more. The warmth and odor of her trembled him.

"Pepito!"

At the sound of Father Moreno's voice Inez pushed Pepito aside with surprising strength and, spurred by guilt, darted over and squatted, taut with apprehension, behind a stack of baskets.

Pepito, momentarily undecided whether or not to respond, went to the doorway and stood there, his long, black-lashed lids blinking against the bright sunlight, an expression of innocence on his youthful, brown face. "You call me, Father?"

"What are you up to?"

"Undressing the corn, Father."

"Is Inez with you?" the priest came toward the storehouse.

"Yes, Father." Pepito turned to Inez. "Father wants you," he said. And forthwith she snatched up an ear of corn and came to the doorway pulling off its husk.

"Good afternoon, Father," she said solemnly, suddenly composed.

Father Moreno came to the doorway and looked inside suspiciously, as if expecting to find some evidence of naughtiness. He then looked at the young faces in turn, as if to say, "What sin have you been committing?" and spoke to the boy: "I want to speak to you in my quarters."

Burning with guilt, Pepito followed the priest down the cloister. Father Moreno seated himself on his bunk and indicated the stool. Pepito sat down.

The priest deliberated how to proceed. "You can't know much about them," he said finally, "because you're too young, but there are many pitfalls, temptations in this life, which, if you expect to go into the priesthood, you will have to avoid. You go through doors," he went on, resorting to allegory, "and they slam behind you. You can't ever get back. Do you understand?"

Pepito's wrinkled forehead denoted confusion. He nodded uncertainly.

The padre cleared his throat nervously, uncomfortable in this delicate situation, and leaned forward, fingertips together and elbows on his skirted knees. "Perhaps I had better put it this way," he said, speaking earnestly, carefully and more sympathetically: "You're just coming into a dangerous age, my son. Nature, which is as relentless as time, is beginning to draw you into her scheme. She cares nothing for your plans or aspirations; all she wants is to use you for her own selfish ends. You must not let her do this. You must be strong in your resistance. You cannot become a man of God and a libertine."

"What is a libertine, Father?"

"A libertine is a seducer, a debaucher, a defiler." And saying these strong words somehow gave the priest a meager pleasure. But seeing that the boy did not understand them, he said, "What I mean is—and we've discussed this before—if you are going to be a priest you'll have to take the vow of chastity. That means you cannot have sexual relations with girls. That is clear, isn't it?"

The boy nodded his lowered head. It was an embarrassing subject.

"Without sex we would not have life, of course," the priest went on, "but sexual relations call for marriage and priests cannot marry."

"Why can't they, Father?"

The question reminded Father Moreno of his instructional days. He had wanted to know the same thing. He found himself quoting his mentor: "When a man is married his interests are divided: his heart, his duty and his loyalty. A priest is an agent of God," he went on earnestly. "He cannot have a wife and children to divide his interests. When one enters the priesthood one gives up one small family for another much larger one—all of mankind." The priest paused to evaluate what he had said. Was he being convincing? Was he keeping the words simple enough? "We are all given this power that is sex," he went on, feeling he had to return to the fundamental topic. "It is a powerful urge and you will find, even after you have become a priest, that you are never entirely free of its pressure. But by renouncing it you will learn the value of sacrifice. In return you will find a rich reward."

The boy looked at the hard-packed dirt floor, at the padre's big, crooked-toed feet with the great, dirty, ridged toenails in the patched sandals. "Yes, Father."

"When you enter the priesthood you turn your back on worldly things, only to gain everything. When you come to enter the priesthood you will be asked, 'Friend, for what purpose hast thou come?' And you will reply, 'To do Your will, O my God, is my delight and Your law is written in my heart.' Do you know what that law is? It is the pledge of virginity. You will be asked. 'Behold the law under which you wish to serve. If you can observe it, enter: if you cannot, freely depart.' This will be asked of you repeatedly, so that you may not excuse yourself on the grounds of ignorance. And anyone who takes this vow is no longer free to leave the Order or to withdraw his neck from under the yoke of the rule. Chastity is the key word. Others are obedience and poverty and humility. Discipline is a key word and so is penitence. To be a true monk means truly to seek God in order to

82

return to Him from whom one has wandered." In the pause which followed, Father Moreno wondered fleetingly if, in trying to guide the boy into the priesthood he was doing the right thing. Perhaps Pepito was not tough or strong enough. It would be a crushing blow if he were rejected. *If I had it to do over again,* the priest mused, *I think I might become a farmer; as such I think I could serve mankind well.*

"You know, my son," he said to Pepito, "if you go into the Church you must love God. There can be no place in your heart for anything else, neither family nor friends nor anything."

"Cannot I love you, Father?"

"You may have affection for me and, if you're so inclined you may respect me, but your heart will belong exclusively to God. It is the only way you will be able to keep your vow of chastity."

"I will try very hard, Father."

"You are a good boy, Pepito," the priest said, feeling somewhat guilty because of how much the child meant to him. "You're an exceptional boy. That is why I am concerned about you." He paused. The ensuing silence bore heavily upon Pepito, and he squirmed uncomfortably under it. "Inez is a fine girl," the priest continued, speaking more casually now. "I don't mean for you to stop playing with her. That isn't it. Just be careful. You might find yourself trapped, and the priesthood would be lost to you forever." The man got up, rubbed his nose with a thumb and forefinger, and put the other hand on Pepito's shoulder. "Keep uppermost in your mind, my son, the question: Would Christ have done this?"

Pepito arose. "Yes, Father."

"If the answer is no, don't do it."

CHAPTER ELEVEN

Ignacio was a week overdue and there was considerable concern for his safety. It was suggested he may have been waylaid and killed, but Falco said "Not Ignacio. He can take care of himself." Vincenti said that Ignacio might very well have collected the garrison's pay and shipped for home, as he had jokingly threatened. "Not a chance," Pedro said. "He may be an atheist, but he'll do what he says he'll do."

"We'll give him until Saturday," Father Moreno said. "If he doesn't return one of you will have to go find out what has happened to him."

Such action was not necessary, however, for late the next afternoon while vespers was being celebrated, Ignacio appeared astride his horse, leading the heavily-loaded packmules. His arrival caused Father Moreno to bring the ceremony to a hasty conclusion. Priests, soldiers and neophytes hurried to welcome the emissary. Where in Heaven's name had he been? What had kept him?

Ignacio reported that he had reached San Diego without mishap and had called at once on Lieutenant Ortega, commandant of the Presidio, who had received him warmly and had treated him to several potations while they discussed the state of military affairs in California.

"Did you get our pay?" Jose asked impatiently.

He had, of course, inquired about that, Ignacio said, but the Commandant had kept plying him with aguardiente and somehow, after a while, the matter became unimportant. The Commandant's wife, whom all the soldiers recalled with pleasure as being comely and plump with a slight moustache, had been very hospitable, providing him with provender and a couch. In the morning he had called at the Mission San Diego and delivered to the resident priests greeting from their brothers at San Juan Capistrano. As to his request for specified goods and supplies, the padres at San Diego were sympathetic but pointed out that they, too, had been ignored by the keepers of the Pious Fund. They had sent what they could spare of cloth and tools and spices.

"What about our pay?" José insisted.

"As soon as I got back to the Presidio I asked the Senor Commandant about that," Ignacio said, "this time while I was sober. He became very annoyed and said, 'There is no pay; there has been no pay; and I'll be damned through all eternity, soldier, if I know when there will be any pay.'"

From his peers came a collective groan of disappointment. Vincenti said, "The son of a pig," and "*Perdon, Padre.*"

"I told him," Ignacio said, "that you would be very disappointed if I did not bring back, in lieu of guilders, some *muchachas* or *liquores*. And he said, 'Ah, it is the same with troops the world over!'" Parenthetically Ignacio said, "He is a great philosopher, this Commandant." Then, "'As for the women; he told me, 'I can't help you. The procurement of a woman is up to the individual and there is not much choice. Other than Indian *putears*, whom you know very well you are forbidden to touch, there isn't an unmarried woman in San Diego. Now as to *liquores*, I might be able to do something—not much, but something. I will see.'" Ignacio paused for dramatic effect and then continued: "I told him if I return to San Juan empty-handed I would be as good as dead. And he told me we were not the only ones who had not been paid. None of the troops at San Gabriel or San Carlos have received a *real*, he said. I told him to come tell you that," Ignacio went on. "I said you would not be inclined to believe me. 'Well,' the Commandant said, 'perhaps I can scrape up a few guilders worth of aguardiente, enough to pacify them.'"

The long and short of it was, Ignacio told his eager listeners: the Commandant gave him twenty guilders, which was not a month's pay for one man, and said that was as much as he could do. He said he was depriving himself and his wife, taking the money from his wife's own impoverished purse, so help him God! But he hoped it would assuage the soldiers at San Juan until the Government of His Majesty the King could get around to paying them. Ignacio said he had no way of knowing whether the Commandant was lying about the pay or not. "For all I know," he said, "he may have diverted our funds to his own purse. Such dishonesties go on. What could I do? I accepted the money, figuring a little was better than none. Besides which my father taught me never to decline money, no matter the circumstances. 'It may be the root of all evil,' he told me, 'but unless you are a priest you can't get along without it.' Now I was in a quandary," Ignacio went on: "how to get for twenty guilders all I'd been asked to bring back. There was, it seemed to me, but one way." Again he paused for effect, looking from one attentive face to another.

"What did you do?" hopefully.

"I wagered it."

"What happened?"

"Lost it all on the turn of the first card."

"Sacred name of God!"

"I had begged," Ignacio went on with a shrug, "now I resorted to borrowing. I had two kegs of aguardient packed on a mule when they caught me. I was in the calaboose ten days before the Commandant turned me loose. It is a very nice place, the calaboose. I have come to have an affection for it. I'd be there yet had the Commandant not learned that I liked it. There is one thing a jailer hates, and that is to have a prisoner enjoy himself. He was furious when I set the jail roof on fire. That was when he decided to get rid of me."

Now here he was, safe and sound, with most of the things the padres needed and greeting to all from their countrymen in San Diego.

"And the aguardiente?" His listeners' mouths were agape awaiting an answer.

Ignacio shrugged again, an elegant, confident shrug which said so much so well, and turned to unpack a mule. "I did my best," he said.

Ensued a brief silence. Then such a wailing went up that the Indians present surmised someone had died. Why had he gambled? Twenty guilders worth of aguardients was better than none at all. It was *their* money he had lost: he had no right to risk it.

"What about my boots?" Vincenti asked.

"Patch the ones you've got or go barefoot," Ignacio said, and proceeded with the unpacking. "If I had won," he said, "I'd have been a hero, so stop your crying." He threw back a straw mat and revealed on either side of the mules two kegs. The caterwauling gave way to joyous shouting. He had been teasing them!

Ignacio grinned triumphantly. "You didn't really believe I'd come back without it, did you?"

Now where there had been censure was affection, where there had been curses was praise. A miracle had been wrought. How in God's name had he procured the brandy without money?

Ignacio smiled cynically, a sly glint in his gold-speckled brown eyes. He reached into a bag and brought forth three tawny-orange kittens. "These are for you, Father Georgio," he said to the senior priest. "Senor Ortega sent them."

Overjoyed and for a moment speechless with surprise, Father Moreno exclaimed, "God bless you, Ignacio!" and taking two of the mottled fluffs into his arms, he picked up the other by the scruff and held it suspended before Father Trujillo. "You see this, Salvatore? This means farewell to the mice problem."

Of more interest to the younger priest were the vestments their brothers at San Diego had sent: an amice, an alb, a stole, and a chasuble, the last of rich ivory brocade with cloth of gold and with a cross and borders embroidered in gold.

Ignacio held up an almost-new deck of cards and a pair of dice, the latter palmed he confessed from one of the garrison at San Diego. For Falco he had brought a lady's comb studded with silver and brilliants.

"What're you going to do with that, Falco?" Jose asked.

"None of your business."

"Why don't you wear it? It'll look good in your curly hair."

"He's sweet on Consuelo," Pedro said, the words impeded by his hare-lip. "I'll bet it's for her."

The other soldiers laughed.

One of the things Ignacio had brought was a letter from the Father Guardian of the College of San Fernando to Father Moreno. Father Moreno retired to his cell to read it. The letter began by apologizing for the inadequacy and tardiness of monies from the Pious Fund, from which the Missions were financed, and for not having sent a brother to replace Father Moreno. *There is such a demand for missionaries all over the new world, here in Mexico and in Central and South America, that we are pressured on all sides. Please exert your patience a little longer, Dear Brother. We will relieve you as soon as we can.*

About the Indian boy of whom you write, the letter went on, *it has been our experience that the natives of the new world do not have sufficient cultural background to undertake the difficult educational program which leads to priesthood. It would appear that it will take several generations to produce such candidates. However, if you feel that this boy's intelligence and other qualifications are sufficient you might want to send him to us that we may put him in preparatory school and evaluate him. As yet no native of the North American continent has been admitted to our Order, and there are two schools of thought on the subject. One, to which you obviously subscribe, contends that, if some could qualify it would be a fine thing for our Mission program. But there are others who feel our prestige and consequently our influence might be lessened thereby. As for me, I am on your side. What better way to educate the natives than through teachers of their own kind, who will be to them shining examples of what they themselves may become? However, I pray you not to send him until he has at least sixteen years.*

After considering the matter, Father Moreno called Pepito and read that part of the letter to him. "Next year," he concluded, "you will go to Mexico City to school. Let us thank God." And while the kittens played with each other and the hem of the priest's habit, the two knelt, the big man with the black, graying hair and red face and the slender brown youth with the big, pale-soled feet. When they had properly thanked and petitioned God, the boy ran off to tell Inez the news.

He found her with Ignacio. She was standing with her back to the white-washed chapel and the soldier was leaning over her, supporting himself with a hand against the wall. Seeing them thus in conversation, Pepito felt suddenly a strong urge of despair. But he quickly squelched his jealousy by reminding himself that he was going to be a man of God.

"I am going to Mexico to school," he said, speaking to them both, now half emptied of the excitement. "Next year—when I am sixteen. It is in the Father Guardian's letter."

"That's fine," Ignacio said indifferently.

Inez laughed tauntingly.

"What's so funny?" Pepito asked.

Ignacio said, "You got a long way to go. Maybe you ought to get started."

"Look what Ignacio gave me," Inez said, indicating a locket hanging from her neck.

Pepito swallowed to moisten his suddenly-dry throat. "It's pretty," he said.

"Go tell Father Moreno he wants you," Ignacio said.

Pepito turned away, obviously dejected. He had expected his friends to be as enthused about his future as he was. Seeing Suegra in the *cocina*, he went thither and imparted his good fortune. "It is a big place," he told her to build up her interest, "with many people and great churches, four or five of them, and lots of ladies and gentlemen in fine clothing who ride about in carriages drawn by horses. They have lights on the streets and sometimes they burn them all night."

"Go away," the wizened old woman said in disbelief. "You take me for a fool?"

"No, it is true," he said. "Father Moreno told me."

Suegra was hardly interested. "I would be afraid to go off to a place like that," she said.

"Why? What's there to be afraid of?"

"Suppose you was to die out there?"

"What difference where you die?"

"You'd be far from home."

"Father Moreno says you'll die when your time comes," Pepito said. "He says that when the Lord wants to take you He reaches down and snatches you wherever you might be."

CHAPTER TWELVE

"*Dominus vobiscum*," Father Moreno said.

Pepito replied, "*Et cum spiritu tuo.*"

They were at the altar. The priest was instructing the boy in the ritual of the Holy Mass, going through the ceremony detail by detail and rehearsing him in the responses.

"Don't slur the Latin, my son. Speak it firmly and enunciate clearly."

"I am afraid of making a mistake," Pepito said.

The priest stifled the urge to smile. "You must learn to say the Latin phrases properly." And he began again the opening words of the Communion: "*Praeceptio salutaribus moniti, et devine institutione formati, andemus dicere. . .*" When he had finished the Lord's Prayer he paused, and the boy said, "*Sed libera nos a malo*," speaking the words loudly and pronouncing them well. They sounded very pleasant.

"*Sed libra nos a malo*—But deliver us from evil," Father Moreno repeated. He was pleased. "That's fine," he said.

At this juncture two persons entered the chapel. Because of the bright sunlight behind them Father Moreno could not at once make out who they were. Then he recognized Falco and Consuelo. "Come in," the padre said.

Falco advanced a few steps. "Could we speak to you, Father?"

"Yes, of course." Pepito slipped outside. "Come sit down."

The soldier took the woman's hand and led her to one of the front benches. Her garment was fresh. She wore the fancy comb in her hair and her face was radiant with that allure nature invests in the young. There was beauty in her docility, in the subtleness of her timidity, in the inheld eagerness which lighted her dark eyes. And for his part, Falco was the young ram brought by some mysterious alchemy to a state of fatuousness. Consuelo sat down beside the soldier, put an arm possessively through his and one bare foot on the other. It was evident why they were there, but the words had to be said, the scene had to be played. And Father Moreno thought idly that this is the female's role, this leading a male into bondage.

"Father—" Falco began and paused, as if reluctant to utter the words that needed to be said.

"Yes, my son."

"Consuelo and I—well, we thought—now that she and Loco have separated—"

Consuelo parenthesized, "Me got baby," proudly, patting her midriff and smirking guiltily. She moved closer to Falco, clinging to his arm and looking worshipfully at his face.

"I assume El Loco is the father." the priest said.

She shook her head.

The scene was so typical of and true to its genre that its pathos caught at the priest's throat. "You mean Falco is the father?"

She nodded extravagantly, looking to the soldier for confirmation. He grinned idiotically, causing Father Moreno to think fleetingly that the male homo sapien is a comic figure at best and, when in love, an utter fool. "What do you want me to do, give you absolution?"

"We want you to marry us, Father," Falco said.

The priest concealed his elation. "What about El Loco?" he asked Consuelo. "Is he not still your husband?"

Quick anger came into her black eyes. "No! No! It is finished. The baby, we want he should be born in the Church."

"Well, I think you should at least discuss the matter with him," the priest said. "If El Loco offers no objection, I shall be happy to see you wed."

"You speak to him, Father," Consuelo implored. "I cannot talk to him."

"Very well. But before I do I want you to know that marriage in the Church is not to be taken lightly. It is a very serious contract. Church marriages are made in Heaven by God and once a couple is united in holy matrimony the wife and husband are inseparable save by death. Marriage is not only an agreement between a man and a woman, it is a sacrament in Christ. Do you understand?"

She nodded uncertainly.

"Furthermore, once you have married Falco in the Church you and he are bound to be faithful to each other. You may not take another man to bed nor he another woman. And if either of you does this, you or he will be committing a mortal sin." Consuelo nodded, looking down at her hands in her lap. Father Moreno thought how pretty in a lascivious way she was, like a work of wanton art. "Do I make myself clear?" he asked, looking from one to the other.

The lovers nodded and Falco said, "Yes, Father."

"If you marry Consuelo, Falco, it is forever, so long as you both shall live."

Consuelo asked timidly: "He can have only one wife?"

"That's right. And you only one husband."

"No sisters?"

"No sisters."

She nodded. "Is good."

"The reason marriage is good," the priest said, "is because together a man and a woman are in harmony with life; together they are productive; together they build and conserve; together they protect each other from the dangers of waste, idleness and temptation. Marriage makes the family and the family is repsonsible for the progress of mankind." Father Moreno stood up. "I'll have a talk with El Loco," he said, helping Consuelo to her feet. "By rights we should get the permission of Falco's commanding officer in San Diego, but under the circumstances," noting the bulge of her belly, "I think we shall forego such a formality."

When they had gone he said to himself: "At least we are making progress," and felt a surge of elation.

When Father Moreno broached the subject, El Loco pretended indifference, but he turned his face so that the priest could not see his expression and kicked at the dust: a sign of displeasure. "You and Consuelo cannot get along," the priest pointed out. "You are always fighting."

"She is bitch dog," the Indian said lightly, as if it were of no importance.

"She is with child. She tells me the child is Falco's. Do you want to take her back?"

El Loco expressed alarm. "Oh, no!" he exclaimed. "I no want."

"It is important the child be born in the Church."

"Women no good."

"That is not true. Treat a woman well and she will more than reward you. What you should do is find yourself another woman and marry her in the Church."

The Indian did not speak for a while but kept kicking the dirt whilst turning the matter in his mind. Finally he said, "You give permission, I go look for wife."

"You have my permission."

El Loco promptly dropped the hoe and set out.

The ceremony which united Consuelo and Falco was touched with that strange sadness which is a concomitant of religious ceremonies, particularly weddings and funerals. As he looked at the two young people standing before him, Father Moreno, bedecked in the newly acquired, gold-embroidered chasuble, had the wistful feeling he always had at weddings. He thought: *It is a ritual civilized man has developed as a bulwark against nature's promiscuity.* He read the hallowed words with the proper solemnity: ". . .to join together this man and woman in holy matrimony, which is an honorable estate, instituted of God in the time of man's innocency, signifying unto us the mystical union that is betwixt Christ and His Church. . ."

The bride's youthful radiance was enhanced by trust and hope and expectancy. She was arrayed in an ecru gown sashed with wild flowers, the short train of which was carried by two button-nosed brown cherubs with wild roses in their hair; and she was further adorned by the silver comb and by necklaces and braclets of beads and shells. Falco had scrubbed and oiled himself to a high shine. He strutted about like a preening bird and it was obvious that he considered himself much more important than his bride. He had waxed his moustache so that the ends stood up, and this made a great change in his appearance. Indeed, he was almost handsome. Father Moreno thought: *To enhance his ego, every man seems to need someone to look down upon, but a wife is hardly a proper subject.*

Throughout the ceremony the natives sat transfixed, not fully comprehending its meaning but properly impressed by its gravity and pomp. The men found it difficult to understand that a man could have but one wife and be obliged to live with her whether he liked her or not. To them, these stipulations were contrary to the laws of nature and so were absurd beyond credence. In their culture, a man married to spend himself in a woman when he felt so inclined, to have her wait on him, to have her keep him warm, and to have someone available on whom he could take out his frustrations. What else, dear God, was a woman for? She had to be of some account to compensate for her incessant chatter and her proclivity for having children. On those scores, women were a damned nuisance.

The wedding was an excuse for a *fiesta*, and following it there was a feast of barbecued fish and there were music, dancing and games. The bridegroom's fellow soldiers, emboldened by arguardiente, made the usual vulgar remarks anent the newlyweds. Gorged on pitahayas, the natives put on a farting contest which had everyone except Father Trujillo, who thought it disgusting, aching with laughter.

The party went on and on into the night and several times during it Vincenti of the big buttocks went behind the chapel to relieve himself. Once while doing so, he became aware in the darkness of another's presence. A woman's voice said, "You want drink of *islay*, maybe?

"Is that you, Suegra?" Vincenti asked.

"*Si.*" She extended a narrow-necked pot. "Is good," she said. "I make."

Islay was the fermented juice of the peyote cactus; it had a wild bitter taste but was highly esteemed by the Indians, it being their only intoxicant. Vincenti accepted the vessel, took a long draught, and might have emptied it had not Suegra snatched it from his mouth. "That's enough!" she hissed sharply.

Saying, "*Gracias,*" he started to move away, but she caught his thick, hairy arm. "You nice," she said. "You I like."

He put his head around the corner of the chapel to see if anyone was coming, then to distract her said, "They're going to start the *takersia.*"

Still holding onto his arm, she put a hand on his genitals. "What you say?—You want girl, maybe? You want maybe I let you have Inez?"

Vincenti's interest was aroused; his attitude changed. "Inez?"

"Be nice to me, I let Inez out tonight."

At that juncture Inez, screaming shrilly, came running around a corner of the chapel and almost collided with Vincenti. "Oh!" the girl inhaled, surprised; and a moment later Pepito ran up and enclasped her. Inez, suddenly angry, slapped Pepito fiercely and, released, dashed away laughing mockingly. The chase was on again.

At midnight Mass was celebrated. Suegra then locked up her charges. The other neophytes went to their wickiups, the priests and soldiers to their bunks. Only Vincenti remained beside the fire's dying embers. The night was soft and fragrant with incense. The crescent moon was high and starlight pierced the shroud of night as through a thousand needleholes. Presently the sound of footsteps preceded Ignacio into the dim light.

"Why are you not in bed, fat boy?"

"I'm not sleepy," Vincenti said. "What are you doing up this late?"

Ignacio sat down on a rock, "We never will know how late it is until it is too late. You need to die for the night, fat boy. Go dream your dreams."

"I wish you wouldn't call me fat boy."

"Why not? You are a fat boy."

"Well, I don't like it."

Ignacio was in a mellow, expansive mood. He stood up and bowed from the waist. "I beg your pardon, my sensitive friend. I am handsome, but I do not resent being referred to as beauty-boy, if there is affection in it."

"Aren't you going to bed?" Vincenti asked.

"Not tonight, skinny one. Tonight I have a tryst with a goddess and she is going to help me plant a people crop."

"You don't make any sense."

"There's no poetry in your big ass, and you have the odor of an onion fart. Get thee gone; go hide your head in slumber."

"I believe you're trying to get rid of me."

Ignacio leaned back and looked up at the sparking canopy of night. "You're clairvoyant. Tell my fortune."

"You're drunk."

"With virtue, my skinny friend, enforced virtue, and badly needing a drain. Pull the plug and posterity will rise all over the world."

"Bullshit."

"Only the attuned ear can appreciate good music."

Vincenti studied Ignacio's long-chinned, sharp-nosed face. In the shadow of his craggy brow Ignacio's gold-flecked eyes caught the firelight and microscopically reflected it. "You got a drink maybe?" Vincenti asked.

"The only things I have to drink are the fresh air and the blood of Christ, and there's damned little of the latter. Would we had His inexhaustible jug."

"You're a blasphemer," Vincenti said. "You're going to end up in

Hell."

Ignacio chuckled. "There isn't any such place," he said. "And you can quote me. The only hell I know of is hunger." Then, after gazing reflectively for a while at the glowing embers he said, "It is better we don't know what time it is. What would you do if you knew you were going to die tomorrow?"

"Who knows? Get drunk, I guess. Anyway, I ain't going to die," Vincenti said, trying to kill the conversation.

"How do you know? Every moment takes you closer to the brink beyond which there is nothing but darkness; and you never know when the next hour is going to be your last. Out of darkness into darkness, and damned little light between."

Vincenti had given up trying to fathom such talk. He sighed disappointedly and settled back. A breeze tussled the young fruit trees, flickered the embers and swirled the smoke. From all about them came the noises of night: frog croaks, cricket stridulations, the crackle of fire. A spark drew a curve across the darkness and dropped to extinction. "See that?" Ignacio asked.

"See what?"

"That spark. It is like a man's life. He is shot out of a woman, goes glowing through life and subsides." When Vincenti did not comment, Ignacio went on: "You're liable to catch cold, sleeping on the ground."

Vincenti did not reply, but lay, hands behind head, looking up at the star-speckled darkness.

Ignacio deliberated. Should he wait until his companion was asleep or should he tell him the situation and ask his cooperation? "*Vincito*," he said finally, leaning forward and speaking quietly and with more affection, "do me a favor?"

"What's that?"

"Go to bed."

"Why?—Why should I?"

"Because I ask you."

"I got as much right here as you have," the fat one said stubbornly.

"Didn't I bring you the brandy?"

"So what?"

"And you won't do this for me?"

"No."

Ignacio sat back, exasperatedly folded his arms across his chest and crossed his legs. "You always were a stupid bastard," he said.

Vincenti raised his head. "What's gnawing on you?"

"Have I got to paint you a picture? Can't you see I'm waiting for somebody. And she is not going to appear as long as you're here."

"Who're you waiting for?"

"None of your business."

Vincenti sat up slowly. "Why didn't you say so?" he asked and got to his feet. Looking down at his companion and slapping the dust off his buttocks, he whispered woundedly, "I'm waiting for somebody, too."

Ignacio was startled.

Vincenti said, "You're always calling me stupid. How about yourself?"

Ignacio got up quickly and caught the fat soldier's arm. "I'm sorry, *Vincito*. It never occured to me."

"I'll take a walk," Vincenti said begrudgingly, and turned into the darkness.

Ignacio slapped him on the back, said, "Thanks, *amigo*," and stood listening as Vincenti's flatfooted steps faded off. He stretched his ears to catch every sound. Now quickly and softly he crossed to the *monjerio*, where, standing before the shuttered window, he whispered, "Mama!" and waited, his breath held, listening.

Came the sound of movement inside. He heard the latch being drawn, slowly to prevent noise, then the door opened a little, Inez slipped out. Ignacio took her hand and they moved through the darkness on tiptoes, going down the cloister toward the river gate.

When Vincenti came back to the fire the coals were deep in ash. He stood for a few hesitant, indecisive moments peering through the darkness at the pale white-washed facade of Father Trujillo's quarters, his puffy face made grotesque by the underlighting. Then, with a confidence-building hitch of his breeches, he crossed to the *monjerio* and tapped gently on the shutters. "Mama Suegra!" he whispered huskily. No response being forthcoming, he tapped again. "Mama!—It's me, Vincenti!"

One of the window shutters, opened from the inside, banged loudly against the wall, and from the blackness came Suegra's angry voice: "Go from here!" uttered with startling volume.

"It's Vincenti!" the soldier whispered, cowed by the disturbance.

The woman cried, "Padre!" as she had been told to do under such circumstances. And almost at once Father Trujillo's sharp voice answered her.

"But," Vincenti whispered, "you promised me."

"Go away," Suegra said.

Came the patter of sandals, the light of a candle and Father Trujillo's voice: "Who's there?" Vincenti, stunned, befuddled and disappointed, was incapable of flight. "So it's you, Vincenti?" Father Trujillo held the candle before the soldier's big, guilty face. "What are you doing here at this hour?"

"He try to get in," the woman said.

Vincenti started to protest but could not think of how to say it; he wanted to tell of the injustice that was being done him, but he did not dare. Father Trujillo said. "It's that liquor!" disgustedly, as if singlehanded he had to stem the tide of evil. "*Va*," he said, and gave the soldier a shove. "Get thee to bed."

CHAPTER THIRTEEN

Father Moreno christened the female kittens Concha and Lola, after his favorite saints, and the male Frasquito, for Saint Francis. The fluffs slept in the priest's room and relentlessly followed him about. Frasquito had, as the Chinese say, a clock in his head. Every morning he would awaken at dawn and leap onto Father Moreno's bed, followed by Lola and Concha, whereupon there would ensue a profuse demonstration of affection.

Af for Father Trujillo, he avoided the kittens as if they were venomous. The first time Frasquito, on a reconnaissance, led his sisters into the younger priest's room he chased them out and protested to his superior: "Father, I must ask you please to keep those cats out of my quarters. They give me the hives."

Father Moreno apologized and proceeded at once, even while Father Trujillo was yet there, to teach the kittens to respect the prelate's wishes. "Father Trujillo," he told them, speaking with mock gravity, "has an antipathy for beasts of your ilk. He considers you souls from purgatory, whereas in truth and in fact you are angels from Heaven. Please, henceforth, eschew him." The senior priest raised a gnarled and dirty-nailed forefinger and held it in front of Frasquito's exquisitely designed little nose. "Don't you ever let me catch you going into his room again. Do you hear?" Then as the kitten cuffed at his finger, he said, "You know, Salvatore, you should really examine your motives. Somehow you seem never able to take the miracle of life as it comes and enjoy it. Always you go protestingly, seeking the shade where there is sunlight, the worm in the great oak. It is sad." Father Moreno then spoke again to the kitten: "I tell him this for his own good."

Father Trujillo said, "Sometimes I can't tell when you're joking and when you're not."

"It is best to assume that I am serious."

"Well, I would prefer you speak directly to me rather than

99

through the cat."

At this point El Loco appeared in the doorway. With him was a flat-chested, skinny woman he introduced as Chuca, his new woman. For an Indian she was fastidiously dressed in a deerskin, poncho-like garment and a meticulously crafted skirt made of hundreds of bits of multicolored reeds strung on flaxen threads. When she walked, the beads made a sassy rustle. Her mannerisms were overly feminine and affected. El Loco told the priests that he would take Chuca to wife and that they would like to have a Church wedding. Father Moreno said he would be happy to unite them in holy matrimony once Chuca had been properly instructed and baptized.

When they had gone, Father Trujillo said, "Did you notice anything odd about that woman?"

Father Moreno picked up Frasquito. "She is very skinny," he said.

"She's coquettish, like a lady at the King's court, Why, she's almost civilized!"

"I hope she exerts a civilizing influence on Loco," Father Moreno said, and raising the kitten, dropped him upside down into the skirt of his habit. The kitten landed on his paws. "Wonderful thing about cats," the older priest said, picking Frasquito up and dropping him again, "no matter how you toss them, they always land on their feet."

"Reminds me of El Loco," Father Trujillo said wryly, and departed.

El Loco and Chuca built their wickiup at some distance from the other Indian shelters. Here Chuca stayed when she was not employed in the fields; and even in the fields she worked apart from the other women, none of whom showed a disposition to associate with her. El Loco resumed his duties as *alcalde*, herding the neophytes through the daily routine. At first Chuca did not attend the religious activities and Father Trujillo questioned El Loco about this: "Doesn't she want to join the Church and learn about God?"

"Oh, yes," the Indian said, and did a little dance to show that everything was quite happy. He was his old, gay, spirited self. Life was a big joke. He picked up a pebble with his toes, transferred it to a hand and threw it over the stockade.

"Then why doesn't she come to church?"

The Indian shrugged in that ridiculously eloquent way he had and said Chuca was shy and that she needed more time to become acclimated.

"Tell her you cannot marry until she has been instructed and baptized. And tell her we can't keep feeding her if she does not join us."

El Loco nodded, did a few more dance steps, twirled about and said, "Maybe so," a phrase which, though he did not quite understand its meaning, he had learned could be uttered effectively almost anywhere in a conversation. That evening he brought Chuca to vespers. She came plastered with pigments and wearing around her boney neck a garland of flowers. The two seated themselves in the rear of the chapel.

For her benefit Father Trujillo told the story of Mary, Mother of Jesus, and went on to quote from Luke: "The Angel Gabriel was sent from God into a city of Galilee called Nazareth to a virgin. . .and the virgin's name was Mary. And the Angel being come in said unto her: 'Hail, Mary full of grace, the Lord is with thee; blessed art thou among women'." He also quoted the woman who said to Jesus: "Blessed is the womb that bore thee and the paps that gave thee suck." And he tried in every way to impress upon Chuca, and incidently the others, the value of virtue and the beauty of womanhood. "Women," he said, "are the incubators of man and therefore the blessed of God."

At the conclusion of the service, both Fathers Trujillo and Moreno went to Chuca to reassure her and to make her feel welcome and secure. "We are pleased to have you here," Father Moreno told her. "El Loco is a good man. He has embraced the Christian faith and the wisdom of God. If you do the same you can be married in the Church and your children can grow up as children of God."

Overwhelmed by this attention, Chuca put her hands to her face and fled. El Loco made a gesture of hopelessness and took out after her.

Father Trujillo asked Consuelo: "What is the matter with her? She is not like the rest of you."

Consuelo avoided the question. "I do not know her," she said. "She comes from another *rancheria*."

So the priest asked Birdwing, and the old man said, "She is a *coia*."

"She's a what?"

"A *coia*."

"What is that?"

"A man who pretends to be a woman."

The startled priest's eyelids blinked several times quickly. "You mean, Chuca is a man?''

Barto shrugged. "There's one in every tribe," he said, as if it were a matter of small importance.

"I confess," Father Moreno said quickly, "I suspected it."

"Heaven wants none such!" Father Trujillo said, irate. "You know what I think? I think El Loco did this on purpose. He is mocking us. He is mocking the Church! He is mocking God! They both should be cast out!"

"We are all God's children," Father Moreno said. "And before we act so drastically, we must establish whether or not Birdwing speaks the truth. Great harm would be done if we punish them and they are innocent."

The priests discussed the matter with Ignacio. "You've had experience with women," Father Trujillo said. "Perhaps you could approach her."

"Are you suggesting I seduce her, Father?"

"Heaven forbid!" the younger priest exclaimed.

"What if she is a female?"

"Then come away at once."

It was deemed prudent to delay the investigation until El Loco was absent, so Father Moreno dispatched him to catch fish. As soon as he was safely away, Ignacio, with Pedro and the other soldiers hiding nearby and the padres watching from behind the Mission stockade, went to Chuca's hut and ducked inside the flap door. Five minutes passed without sign or signal. Father Moreno said, "She must be a woman or he'd be out by now."

"She may have killed him."

"Not in so short a time," Father Moreno said wryly. And as he spoke Ignacio's back pushed the curtain aside. It was evident he was trying to pull Chuca into the open. He lost the advantage briefly and disappeared again, only to reappear with an arm locked about the Indian's head. The latter fought furiously, kicking out a portion of the hut in desperation. And now there was no doubt as to the Indian's sex: it was male. He tried desperately to hide his genitals with his hands, but the other soldiers, hastening to help Ignacio, took his arms and twisted them behind him, exposing him for all to see.

The priests came out to confront him. Father Trujillo cried: "Shame on you, you dreadful sinner!" and addressed the assembled neophytes: "Look at him—trying to hide the lie!"

"You dogs!" the skinny Indian snarled. "You lice-bitten dogs!"

And he spat and pawed the ground. His ribs were prominent and his thin chest was spotted with irritations caused by his having pulled hairs out by their roots.

Father Trujillo slapped his face hard. "Don't you spit at me!" And now other Indians pressed forward and began taunting Chuca. The children, not entirely understanding the situation but aroused by the derision, stuck out their tongues at him; and one small child, confused by the excitement, hit him with a rock.

Father Moreno addressed the assembled: "You have all seen this man going about pretending to a woman," he said. "That is a venal sin. It is dishonest and it is indecent and it will not be permitted here." Now he spoke to Chuca: "Get your belongings and go. You are a disgrace to your people." He spoke to the soldiers: "Let him go."

Released, the naked man covered himself with his hands. The other Indians, partly to please the padres and partly because they liked to assume authority, shouted torments at him and commanded him to vamoose.

"I wait for Loco," Chuca said pleadingly.

"You will go now. At once."

Pedro laid his leather whip across Chuca's back. "Do what you're told."

Chuca snarled at the soldier and ducked back into the hut. He reappeared presently in bead skirt and poncho, came forth shyly, hesitantly, defiantly, taking as much time as he dared and, small bundle in hand, set off up the path toward the mountains, followed by taunts and hurled stones.

When El Loco returned in the late afternoon, Father Moreno went to reprimand him. On the way the priest summoned the necessary choler to sustain him in his duty. Bringing Chuca to the Mission had been a monstrous, even a diabolical thing, he told himself, and it was obvious that El Loco had done it for derision. He probably had the idea, becuse the two missionaries wore skirts, that they, too, were *coias*. . .

He found the Californian squatting outside his hut cleaning fish. El Loco's smile revealed his stumpy teeth. "Good evening, Father," he said, and threw some entrails to a mangey dog. The first wisps of a desert-drawn fog moved past them. "El Loco," the padre said, his voice lacking its usual warmth, "we have sent Chuca away and you will have to go, too. We do not want you here.''

Incredulity and pain came into the Indian's face. "Chuca? Chuca?—'' He straightened and looked about him. "Where is Chuca?''

"I told you: we have sent him away.''

"Why Father? What is trouble?''

"She is a man. You have been living a lie. It is evil. It is against God.''

The Indian stood up. "Chuca, she is *coia*,'' he said matter-of-factly. "She more woman than man. She no hurt nobody.''

"We will not have him here. He is an evil influence.''

El Loco squatted down and resumed cleaning the fish. "He is what he is,'' he said philosophically. Then, struck by an idea, he said, "God make him.'' And now suddenly, as if they had disposed satisfactorily of that subject, he laughed pleasantly and held up the largest bass. "I bring you fish, Father.''

Looking at the puckered, brown, smiling face with the falt, wide-nostrilled nose and big mouth, Father Moreno had the uncomfortable feeling he was being mocked. He said, "You must go, Loco.''

The Indian's smile changed abruptly to a frown. "Me? Why? I no am *coia*.''

"We are trying to teach your people the way of God and you bring Chuca here. You are as guilty as he is. We don't want you here.''

El Loco threw the sculpin he had been cleaning at the dog, which got up and sniffed the fish. The Indian rose and began to rant, speaking in Chumash, damning everything and everybody to a Chumash hell. He said the priests dressed like women; why couldn't a *coia*?

Father Moreno caught him by an arm. "Now see here,'' the priest said, "you stop that!'' The padre's touch was enough to subdue the Indian. He cowed. "Have your supper,'' Father Moreno said, "but I don't want to find you here in the morning.''

After cleaning the fish El Loco went inside the hut, coaxed the ashes to a blaze and proceeded to cook a fish and gorge his stomach, soured by the injustices he felt had been done him. He had been loyal to the padres and had helped them when they needed him; now that he was no longer useful they had cast him out. If that is the way God did things, then God was an ungrateful *chauhuistle*.

His few belongings in a basket he ducked out, entered the Mission by the main gate and groped his way through the fog to the chapel. He would go, but he would take a thing or two with him. All he needed to perform as a priest, he felt, was a costume. He would put the fear of God into his fellow Californians and they would do his bidding.

From the armoir, where the vestments were kept, he removed the glittering chasuble. It would compensate him for the unfair way he had been treated. He donned the garment, tucking its skirts into his breeches, and left the chapel by the side door. The fire in the patio forced a faint glow through the fog. He could hear the plaintive music of a guitar. At another time he would have made his way to the fire and would have danced and played the fool for laughter. But now all of that was denied him. Treading softly, he followed the stone-bordered path to the granary. Here, aside from the corn and wheat and other stores, were kept the harness and saddles. He pulled the leather latchstring, pushed open the door and groped along a wall until he located a halter. Then he found a basket into which he scooped some grain and, hurrying, made his way to the corral gate. He slid the gate bolt back slowly, trying not to make any noise; nonetheless, several of the horses and mules came clumping toward him. He had never entirely overcome a fear of horses, and when one nudged him in the darkness his scalp froze. His terror was compounded when a horse whinnied; the sound all but scared the wits out of him. He moved along the stockade followed by the animals, one of which soon found the grain. The Indian pushed the big head away and whispered, "Mirabel!—Come Mirabel!" in imitation of Pepito. As the horses and mules crowded about him to nibble the grain he felt their faces, and while speaking to God: "Now, God, I've asked you before—I don't know how many times—and You haven't done what I asked You to do. I can't keep asking You to help me if You don't listen. I'm asking You now to help me, and if You don't do it I'm not going to ask You again." Finally—could it be? "Mirabel, is that you?" he whispered, feeling furry whiskers. It was she, and, joyed, he permitted her to poke her nose and jaws into the basket. He managed after several attempts to get the halter over her head; then before leading her out of the corral he stood motionless, listening. Came the reassuring sounds of guitar and song. As for Mirabel, she was docile enough; it was as if she were aware of and approved the felony.

They followed the corral fence to its end. Then El Loco, eager to increase the space between himself and the padres, drew the burro up and set about the unfamiliar business of mounting her. The darkness

105

was a hindrance and so was the chasuble, but now was not the time for hesitation. He leaped up, as he had seen Pepito do, and abruptly found himself in a heap on the beast's other side. Mirabel stood patiently and submissively while he tried again from her right side. This time he was too cautious. The third time he managed to remain on the burro's back, only to discover he had dropped the halter rope. When he reached forward to retrieve it, he lost his balance and slid off. Now from the patio came shouting which El Loco incorrectly assumed was addressed to him. He had failed to close the corral gate securely and the other animals had wandered into the vegetable garden. The shouting was directed at them. El Loco grasped the halter, leaped onto Mirabel's back almost expertly and the burro, satisfied at last the everything was as it should be, set out briskly into the night.

Instinctively she turned south, following the riverbed, taking the path to the nearest Indian village, precisely the place El Loco wanted to avoid because he realized there would be the first place his pursuers would look for him. He wanted to go east, up the canyon which led into the mountains. In an effort to explain this to Mirabel he tugged at her halter and implored her in Chumash. But true to her genus and sex she heeded him not. On she went, impervious, stubborn as destiny, until finally he slid off her, pulled her about, and led her out of the riverbed. There he remounted and urged her into a bumpy, jogging trot. They went bounding along, El Loco hanging onto the lady's furry neck and Mirabel moving maliciously stiff-legged as if she not only understood the situation but relished it.

Presently the fog lessened and eventually they climbed out of it into the clear night. The moon was on the wane, but it gave sufficient light that they were able to discern large objects. They went along this way for a considerable distance, until Mirable, as if on command, stopped and commenced cropping such grass as her nose could find.

El Loco slid off her with a long sigh of relief. Being in no wise disposed to spend the rest of the night there, he tugged at the rope, urging her on. To no avail; she merely extended her neck without moving her feet. Though he pulled with all his strength, planting his heels against a rock, the burro refused to budge. Indeed, it seemed that the harder he pulled the deeper she planted her hoofs. Nor did the rain of Chumash curses he sprayed upon her have any effect. Finally, acutely conscious of the dangers behind him, El Loco changed tactics: "Come, little sweet one," he pleaded, stroking her neck. "It is late. We go." And when this entreaty proved equally ineffective, he looked about for a switch. The piece of greasewood he found broke in two, so he got behind her and pushed. She did not budge. There was something inexorable and capricious, like time, about her, the way she went on eating, oblivious to wheedling, pleading and cursing. At his frustrated wit's end, El Loco for a brief moment contemplated leaving her and making for the hills alone. But the pictured pleasure of riding into a village and lording it over his fellows was irresistible. "Come, mule," he kept saying. "Come, you louse of a dog!" And he smoothed her coat, petting her dishonestly. Now suddenly he leapt upon her back, resorting to surprise to move her, and to his delight the unpredictable burro started slowly, stoically to move ahead, going on up into the hills.

By now the Indian was becoming more accustomed to riding; he even pushed himself to an uncertain sitting position, and, presently by way of experimentation, jabbed the lady with his heels, the way he had seen Pepito do; whereupon she broke into a slow reluctant trot. The trot was not sustained, and after a few dainty steps she resumed a walking pace, ignoring his blunt yells and gruff entreaty.

Then slowly, as if she hoped he wouldn't notice, Mirabel started to turn back. Unable otherwise to redirect her, El Loco dismounted. In doing so he stepped on a cactus. His howl startled the burro and she shied. Surprised to find herself suddenly free, she tossed her head a couple of times, testing, then proceeded to wander in search of grass.

One after another El Loco drew the barbs out with his teeth, taking care not to break them. So engrossed was he in this operation that it was some time before he became aware Mirabel had wandered off. Then panic seized him, and he got up and hobbled about, calling her name pleadingly. At last he discerned her nibbling her way back down the mountain. As he approached, limping, she moved faster, taking a nibble here and there but moving with a purpose, realizing that eventually she would be caught and femalewise enjoying the chase. When finally he caught hold of the rope she stood tractable and polite while he tied her to a bush. Thereafter he renewed his efforts to extract the cactus spines. A number still remained in his foot when he decided he had wasted all the time on the operation he could afford. Breaking off a piece of manzanita, he remounted and urged the burro forward; and each time Mirabel balked or tried to turn back he dissuaded her with the switch. Moving back and forth across the mountainside, ever climbing through the thick brush, they traveled through the night.

It was well after sunup when they came in sight of a lake beside which was a native village. The lake lay like a great blue mirror in a verdant valley surrounded by beautifully proportioned mountains. Thirsty, hungry and weary, Mirabel plodded steadily onward, going down toward the precious water, her rider with the parched throat and swollen, throbbing foot urging her on.

They reached the village at mid-morning and, as they approached the settlement, El Loco arranged the beautiful chasuble so that it was exposed in all its resplendent glory and sat erect, mustering such dignity as he could command.

A tall, boney, awkward Californian came forward and began an harangue. It was evident he and the others clustered behind him were afraid of the burro and distrustful of the clothed stranger. El Loco dismounted and released Mirabel, and the burro went directly to the water and began drinking. Standing, his weight on his uninjured foot, El Loco listened politely. The Chieftain ultimately concluded his remarks by asking El Loco whence he had come and where he was going.

"Before I reply," El Loco said, "I wish to ask permission to drink. I have come a long way and my throat is dry." And hiking the chasuble skirts, he went to the water's edge and, squatting beside Mirabel, scooped water in his cupped hands and drank thirstily and noisily. His thirst slaked, he returned to the Chief and explained he had come from the village of pale men near the sea. He said he had been empowered by them to go forth on the mule to seek converts for the Mission, that indeed he had been gifted by them with peculiar powers to heal the sick and comfort the unhappy. He said he had been granted these powers because he had saved from death one of the pale men who dressed as women. "They do not make children," he told his listeners. "They say we are their children."

Throughout this spiel the listeners' credulous faces were blank with the wonder of what he was saying, and it gave El Loco a feeling of power and strength that they should have swallowed as truth such a collosal lie. He forgot for a moment his hunger, exhaustion and sore foot. Like any orator who feels the drunkenness of spellbinding, he was loath to finish. He told them about the soldiers and their shooting sticks, about the horses and cattle, about the guitar, about growing grain and planting trees to bear fruit and about cards for gambling.

"We have heard about these strangers," the Chief replied, when at last El Loco faltered. "We do not trust them. They have come here to enslave us."

El Loco, ever one to vacillate, agreed: "I do not trust them either," he declared, unaware of any inconsistency. "I have escaped from them and they are trying to catch me. I have come here to live with you. Here they will not find me."

"We are flattered that you have chosen to live with us," the Chief said. "But we must decline the honor. You cannot stay here. We do not want any trouble with the pale men. We do not want the strange beast here, either. Our children are afraid of him."

"You mean the little mule?" El Loco asked, and turned to look at Mirable, cropping the delicious green grass which grew beside the lake. "He is nothing to be afraid of!"

"Won't he bite you?" the Chief asked.

"Oh, no," El Loco said. "Mirabel!" he called, to demonstrate his mastery of the beast. "You, Mirabel!" But the burro's only indication she had heard him was the cock of a swivel ear and the roll of a wary eye. "I will show you how to ride the mule if you will give me something to eat," he said. "I am very hungry."

The Chief spoke to a woman and she detached herself from the throng. "We will give you to eat," the Chief said, "then you must go."

El Loco shrugged. "As you please." he said. "I could tell you many wonderful things I have learned from the pale men. But if you do not want to learn them, that is your loss."

The Chief said, "I have heard some words about these creatures," referring to the burro. "I am told they are mean and treacherous and that their bite is deadly."

"This mule would not hurt a flea," El Loco said. "He is gentle like a dog."

"I hear they kick with their hind paws."

"Such words are wind. This mule is a messenger from the pale man's Chinigchinich. He looks on the laughing side of everything. Thus mule can perform miracles," El Loco went on, gesturing extravagantly. "With him I can make rain and I can chase away evil spirits."

The Chief looked up at the clear, pale sky, whitened by the rising heat, and as he did so the others looked up also. "We could use some rain," the Chief said. "Let us see you make it rain."

"If you will let me and the mule stay with you, we will make it rain," El Loco said. "We will fill up the lake."

"You make rain today and maybe we will let you stay."

"We may not be able to make rain today," El Loco said. "It is a little quick. We have to talk to the gods—maybe they are not ready. Give us a week and we will make rain.'

"If you can make rain," the Chief said, "you can make it any time. Make just a sprinkle now to show us you can do it."

"Oh, we can do it all right, the mule and I. I have learned how from the pale people."

"They can make rain?"

El Loco clapped his big hands. "Like that," he said. "They can do many wonderful things."

"Do they need the mule to make these wonders?"

"Oh, yes. Without the mule they cannot do much."

"How can the mule make rain?"

"I cannot tell you the secret. But I can make him do it all right."

"It is strange the pale people gave you this wonderful creature if he can make rain," the Chief said. "Why did they not keep him to make rain for them? It has been a long, dry season."

"It has not been dry for them," El Loco said. "They have made lots of rain."

"That is hard for us to believe," the Chief said apologetically, not wanting to be rude. "You will have to make just a little rain before we can believe you."

And even while he was still speaking, Mirabel spread her legs a little, raised her brush of a tail and began urinating.

For the moment no one spoke. All gazed, mouths agape as if a miracle were indeed happening before them. Then one of the Indians shouted, "Oh—ho!—so that's how he make rain!" and the others, their awe dispelled, howled with laughter and slapped each other, making a great display of their hilarity.

"It is golden rain!" the Chief cried, between spasms of laughter.

"It is bubbling rain!"

"It will kill the flowers!"

"I have a dog that can make that kind of rain!"

And with each remark the laughter was renewed.

Meanwhile Mirabel stood stoically, a bemused and bored expression on her netherworld face. It was as if she were pleased with what she had done, though a little surprised and somewhat disdainful of the reaction it had elicited.

The woman brought a bowl of atole and El Loco, while the natives plied him with ridicule, proceeded to eat as if the food were to be his last. When he had swabbed the bowl with a finger and had cleaned the finger by sucking on it, the Chief addressed him: "It has been very amusing having you here, we hope you will have a pleasant journey, wherever you go, you and your magical mule."

"I have learned all the pale people know," El Loco said earnestly. "I have learned all about the world, which they say is round, like a ball of mud, and about the stars and about what happens after death. And I can teach it to you if you will let me stay."

The Chief asked, "What comes after death?"

"I will not say unless you welcome me."

Someone cried, "Make it rain again!" and everyone except El Loco laughed.

El Loco's feelings were hurt. He got to his feet, pulled at the chasuble, belched and said, "I will go beyond the mountains and down into the valley and I will make it rain there."

"That is a good place," the Chief said. "It is dry there."

El Loco approached Mirabel with feigned nonchalance, but as he did so she began walking away from him cropping grass as she went.

"Mirabel!" El Loco said, speaking sharply. "Wait for me. We are going." As he increased his speed, she did likewise. It was very embarrassing.

"Mirabel!—you hear me?" And though he did not feel like running, he did so finally, whereupon she stopped and let him come up to her. He led her back a way and proceeded to mount her, though not without difficulty, for the chasuble got in the way. Finally astride her, he addressed the gathering. "I could put a curse on you for refusing me asylum," he said, gesturing. "But I will not do it because I do not want to bring you hardship and misery. I do not want your houses to burn and your enemies to kill you. After I am gone you will be sorry you did not take me in. Then it will be too late. You had a fine chance to control the weather and make the earth give forth its fruits, but you would not take it. I am sorry for you." He reined the burro, turned her around, kicked her ribs, and waved as she moved on, going stoically, restrainedly, like time.

They went but a mile or two beyond the village, following a trail around the lake, before El Loco, hardly able to hold his head up, dismounted. He tied Mirable and lay himself down to sleep.

It was there Pedro and Vincenti, who had been in the saddle all day, came upon him. They were tired and in no mood for words. Without ado, they tied him to a cottonwood and welted him with their belts until their arms were sore. Then they took Mirabel and the chasuble and headed back to the Mission.

"That's the last we'll hear of Loco," Pedro said. "He'll never show his face again!"—a prognostication which proved to be quite wrong.

CHAPTER FOURTEEN

Ignacio sat on a stone bench against the chapel wall, the skin of his eyes puckered against the setting sun. He was watching a hawk hover motionlessly in the dry sky and thinking about Inez. If he married her the padres would be pleased and, according to them, God would like it. God knows, she would be lucky. The hawk closed its wings and, as if sprung from a bow, dove, a streak against the blue, only to brake as suddenly and go swooping back up into the void, again to take up its hungry vigil.

Ignacio mused that one thing lives on another, that but for the dead maggots would starve. And watching a native eat posole, he thought that of the three fundamental functions of man—masticating, defecating and fornicating, only eating is performed in public, though it too can be obscene. He watched from a corner of an eye Inez come out of the monjerio and cross the quadrangle, and when she sat down beside him he pretended not to notice her. Following Indian custom, she could not speak first. Finally he ventured, "Good evening," and she, happy to have her presence noted, replied likewise. Another silence ensued. The evening was warm and purple and fraught with euphoria. A haze scrimmed the scene's blemishes. The one-note scraping of crickets countered the soft music of drum and gourd. As the sun slipped into its slot the cusp of a moon emerged above the lavender bulge in the east like an afterthought.

"You know what is love?" Ignacio asked.

Inez nodded emphatically. "God," she said. "God is love."

"Sure," Ignacio said lamely, not having had that answer in mind. "It's something else, too."

"What?" she asked eagerly.

He extended his two forefingers. Indicating one, he said, "You," and indicating the other. "Me." He then put them together. "That is *amor.*"

She repeated the Spanish word and made a circle of the thumb and forefinger of her left hand and put the forefinger of her right hand through it.

Ignacio was amused. "*Si,*" he said, and looked toward Father Moreno to see if he was observing them. The priest was examining the flourishing grapevines. Beyond him, outside the *cocina* a few men were playing *tousee*. Father Trujillo came out and rang the bell for Angelus. The music ceased. Everyone bowed his head in silent prayer, after which Suegra called to her charges: "Come, come, little virgins, the night is nigh!"

Inez got up. Ignacio put a hand on her arm. "Tonight?" She shook her head and went running across the quadrangle. As she disappeared into the monjerio Ignacio made up his mind to speak to Father Moreno. He got up and approached him thinking: *A priest settles disputes, listens to grievances and excuses, administers to the sick and the sick-at-heart; he encourages and restrains, judges and punishes, enlightens and guides. Woes and wails are his daily fare. From a priest's point of view the layman's life is made up of peccadillos, iniquities, injustices, complaints and delusions.*

"Pretty soon, wine, eh Father?"

"God willing."

"Grapes look good."

"If the Indians and the birds don't steal them all before they ripen, we should have a good crop." Then, struck by a sudden thought, the priest said, "Bacchus would be a good name for you, Ignacio. If you had cloven hoofs you would be his image."

Ignacio grinned, pleased. "Father, I've been thinking I ought to take a wife."

Father Moreno lifted a caterpillar off a vine, dropped it on the ground and squashed it with his sandal. It made a moist blob in the dust. "So!—"

"It looks as if I'm going to be here a long time."

"I assume you have Inez in mind."

The soldier nodded.

"Is she pregnant?"

Ignacio looked hurt. "Now, Father—"

"Of course, if she were you could swear it wasn't your doing. You could blame it on Vincenti."

"I'm serious, Father."

"I suppose she's willing?"

"I think so. Yes."

"I'll have to prepare her," the priest said.

"If I marry her, Father, and they send me home: would I have to take her with me?"

"A marriage is a marriage. In sickness and in health, until death."

114

The finality of this statement appeared to give Ignacio pause and Father Moreno thought he should act before the soldier changed his mind. "I can have her ready by Sunday," he said.

"I never thought we'd see the day," Jose said.

"He got a hard on," Pedro said.

"He ain't the only one," Vincenti said. "I think I'll marry one of these *muchachas* myself."

"Where you gonna find one who'll have you?"

Male talk: irreverent, insulting. To these men, marriage meant uninhibited sex and little else; that it might entail the magic of love did not occur to any of them.

Little of the day's light was left when a lone traveler appeared leading a mule: a tall, thin, bearded man with abnormally large gnarled hands. Travelers, of course, were always a source of excitement and the padres, soldiers and Indians gathered at the main gate to welcome him. Father Moreno thought he detected in the stranger's fierce black eyes a disquieting fanaticism.

"I am called Jesus Echeverria," the bearded man said. "I am a stone mason and I have been sent by the College of San Fernando to build a church here."

Overjoyed, Father Trujillo exclaimed, "God has answered our prayers!"

Pepito looked after the weary mule and the padres escorted the mason to the *cocina*. Father Moreno suggested that, to ease the weariness of his long journey, Jesus might like a dram of brandy, but the latter declined, saying, "I do not take strong drink." without adding the conventional *gracias*. He accepted bread and cheese and a gourd of goat's milk, and while he ate he told the priests that he had been working on a church in Mexico City when the call came to proceed to California. "God sent me," he said. He had come to San Diego by ship from San Blas bringing with him his masonry tools. "I am going to build God the most beautiful church in all of California," he said. And he and the priests talked well into the night about plans for the church and about the state of the world from which he had come.

If the mason was ungracious and boastful, he compensated for

115

these characteristics by being an indefatigable and zealous worker. Although he did not get to sleep until very late that first night, he set out at dawn the next day to scour the countryside in search of suitable building stone. Eventually he discovered a deposit of good to excellent limestone in a hillside about three miles north of the Mission and began to teach the natives to quarry and cut the stone, a task at which he himself worked every day from sunup to sundown. "He seems possessed," Father Moreno said to Father Trujillo.

The stone blocks were brought to the building site in *carretas* and by women and children carrying them on their heads. Watching the ant-like line of Californians strung out over the countryside, Father Trujillo observed: "Each is doing his part for the glory of God." To which Father Moreno added, "And for the prizes of beads, clothing and blankets. It is sad that man's avarice comes before his spirituality."

Father Moreno was at prayer, kneeling before his bunk, when there came a knock on his door. He opened it to find Jesus who appeared to be in a highly excited state. The flickering light of Father Moreno's candle gave the mason's bearded face a ghoulish look.

"Father, I have something to tell you."

"Come in."

The priest let the hot wax drop on the table and planted the candle in it then sat down on the bunk. Jesus, seating himself on the stool, seemed undecided how to phrase his announcement. After a long pause he said, "It is of the utmost importance." Father Moreno nodded. Jesus looked around. "We are alone?"

"Yes. Except for the cats."

Another pause before Sebastian said, "I'm wondering if you will believe me?"

"Why should you lie to me?"

"Oh, I wouldn't, Father."

"What's on your mind." And, thinking the man wanted to confess, the priest asked, "Have you sinned?"

"Oh, no!" The bearded man shook his head. In the silence that followed could be heard the yapping of coyotes and the hoot of an owl. Father Moreno waited. Finally the mason blurted, "What would you say if I told you I am Jesus Christ reincarnated?"

The priest blinked, his mouth opened involuntarily and he

swallowed a knot in his throat which caused his prominent Adam's apple to bob up and down.

"I am the promised Second Coming," the mason said.

"When did you find this out?"

"Just now. God told me. I've suspected it for some time. My mother's name was Maria. She never married. And she told me that God was my father. That's why she named me Jesus. I have always known that I was different from other people."

Father Moreno thought: *The man is crazy*. He said, "When God spoke to you, what did He say?"

"He said, 'You are my only begotten son, Jesus Christ. I have sent you back to the world to rid it of sin. I want you to go forth and heal the sick, cleanse the lepers, comfort the poor and free the oppressed'."

Not wanting by his expression to reveal his disbelief, Father Moreno sat up so that his face was in shadow. "Does it occur to you as strange that God would send you away out here where the only sins are the sins of ignorance, where there are no lepers, no oppressed, no rich and so no poor? I should think that He would have revealed this startling news to you while you were in Mexico where you would have had a fertile field to work in."

The priest's logic confused the mason momentarily, but he quickly recovered. "My Father works in wondrous ways," he said. There was spittle in the corners of his fringed mouth.

"Did He tell you how to go about doing all those things?"

"No. But he has directed me to you. You are wise in the ways of sin. You have been fighting the dragon all your life. I want you to be my first disciple."

"I am overwhelmed by the honor," the priest said, "but I am surprised He did not send you to the Pope. Your returning to earth is such a momentous event one would think God might have heralded it."

"There was no fanfare when I was born in Bethlehem."

"There was the star."

"When God spoke to me I saw a bright light. It was dazzling."

"You being Jesus," Father Moreno said, "I wouldn't presume to give you advice, but if I were you I'd wait for God to tell me how to proceed before disclosing my identity. If people don't believe you are Jesus reincarnated you could become an object of ridicule. Be content to live as Jesus lived, without sin, and by your example you will inspire everyone. I am sure that is what God wants you to do."

"But He told me to go forth and convert."

"You are doing God's work by building His house. It is important that you continue." And while the mason reflected on this, the priest went on: "Bide your time. God will show you the way." Soothing words, spoken as to a disappointed child.

The mason looked up, encouraged, and again Father Moreno saw that strange, wild look in his eyes. "And you will be my disciple?"

"I will be your disciple. Now," the priest said, "let us ask our Heavenly Father to guide us. . ."

CHAPTER FIFTEEN

Father Trujillo arose from his bunk at the first light of day, got up quickly as if sleeping were a sin, dashed cold water from a basin on his face, wiped it off with a cloth made gray by many washings with impure soap, took a mouthful of water, worked it through his stubby teeth, and spat it out on the way to the community toilet. Later he stood before the cross in the patio and recited his office. Beyond the profiled mountains to the east the pale glow of morning was lightening. A scrawny dog got up from his bed beside the cookhouse, stretched ecstatically and stood wagging his tail meekly, uncertainly; now he yawned, opening his jaws impossibly wide, and stood looking sleepy-eyed as if he hadn't just performed a small miracle. From the mud-fenced corral a rooster crowed, his arrogant tidings breaking the clockless silence. And thereafter it was as if the world had stopped: neither the sound of a heartbeat nor the whisper of a breeze.

His devotion reaffirmed, Father Trujillo grasped the bellrope and, with grim satisfaction, pealed the Angelus. "Up! Up!" he cried, his eyes alight with zealous pleasure at thus arousing sinners from their beds. "Up!—and to God's work!"

Father Moreno turned on his bullockhide bed and curled himself under the blanket like a great fetus, instinctively withdrawing from the disturbance. He had been at home with his sister. For some reason it had been necessary that he go upstairs, but the stairway had been removed. He had dragged a table into the entryway and placed a chair thereon. From the chair he had tried to pull himself up by two rungs of the balustrade. The rungs had given way. . .

Frasquito was cuffing him on an ear. The priest sat up, still more asleep than awake, a comical figure with the fringe of his head hair sticking up at all angles, the skin of his big, stubbled face heavy with sleep, his coarse gray nightshirt open at the throat. A shiver passed through him. He stretched, yawned, rubbed his nose and spoke to the kittens: "We die and we come to life again, we die and come to life. It

119

is a miracle which happens every day." The clangor of the bell and the strident voice of Father Trujillo caused Father Moreno to observe: "Our dear brother's greatest delight, I do believe, is in rousing us." He fumbled for his sandals, shuffled his big feet into them, stood, stretched agonizingly and, observing his dirty fingernails, resolved that day to clean them. Standing in the doorway, he looked upward at the gray sky and said, "Good morning, God," cheerfully. Then, frowning, he shouted a less cheerful greeting to his fellow priest, "Desist, Salvatore, or you will wake the dead."

"Rise, rise! It is Saint Polycarp's day!"

"The way you're ringing the bell it sounds more like Christmas."

Consuelo came through the main gate leading Maria Magdelena by a hand. Released, the child ran to the older priest. He squatted, caught her in his hands and lifted her up, saying, "Upsadaisy!"

The child said, "Morning, Father," speaking in Spanish, and opened her legs about his waist. The while hugging him, she squirmed her pelvis against him in a lascivious way.

"How is my little angel?" Father Moreno asked, pretending not to notice her precociousness.

"Muy contento, gracias."

The priest kissed her on a cheek and put her down. At once, on a whim, she left him to chase a chicken. He was pleased with the way she spoke Spanish. The ease with which she had learned the language made her an object of considerable amazement to the other natives. How, they asked, can a mere child do something which adults find so difficult? The padres said it was a gift from God, and Consuelo, because of her child's bilingual talent, had come to think of herself as one apart, as if she had borne a saint.

The kitten Concha had followed Father Moreno out the door, and now he picked her up, preparatory to putting her back inside. "Do you realize, little one, that over yon hill soon will come God's greatest miracle, the faithful sun?" And even as he spoke a young woman went by, her belly bulging with a babe. The priest wished her a good day, then readdressed the kitten: "And there goes God's *second* greatest miracle." He put the kitten inside and closed the door.

One by one the sleepy-eyed Indians and half-dressed soldiers straggled into the little chapel and took their places on the rough hewn benches. Father Moreno, wearing a cope, recited the morning prayer; and though the Latin was incomprehensible to the Indians, they sat through the ceremony dutifully and somewhat awefully. And when it ame time for the recitation of the Doctrine Christiana—the Sign of the Cross, the Lord's Prayer, the Hail Mary, the Apostle's Creed, the Confiteor, the Acts of Faith, Hope, Charity and Contrition, and the Ten Commandments of God—the natives joined in as best they could, repeating those phrases which were familiar to them and mumbling those which they had not memorized. After the *Alabado* and the *Cantico del Alba* had been sung, Father Moreno took up the Padron, a book in which were recorded the name and date of birth of each neophyte. As he began the roll-call he sensed a furtiveness among the congregation and was aware of nudgings and sly glances. To prevent one from answering for another when a name was called, each was obliged to come forward and kiss the priest's hand. If one was absent a reasonable excuse was required. Thus as Father Moreno progressed and Cueras, Estaban, Hermano, Juan, Pujo, Tomas and Zambo did not respond there was cause for concern. And when the priest asked if anyone knew where these men were, members of their families dropped their eyes and shook their heads. "This is most unusual," Father Moreno said. "Could it be that all are sick?" And when there was no answer, he addressed Pujo's wife, sitting in the front row. "Clarita, is Pujo sick?"

Pressed thus, Clarita said, "Yes, Father, he is sick."

Father Moreno sent Pepito to check the missing men. "If they are sick they should be administered to." He well knew that the replies he had from Clarita and the others were unreliable.

As a rule when pressed with captious questions, the natives either pretended not to understand or gave the reply the questioner expected. They feared the truth might cause embarrassment and embarrassment to them was painful.

Father Moreno kept the neophytes in the chapel until Pepito returned. The boy reported that he had been unable to find any of the absentees. Whereupon the priest questioned Lola, Estaban's wife, she being more proficient in Spanish than the other woman. "When did you last see Estaban, Lola?"

The woman hung her head. "In the night," she replied.

"He was not there this morning?"

She shook her lowered head.

"Has he gone off with the others?"

"I don't know."

"He did not tell you where he was going?"

She shook her head, still without looking up.

121

"Where do you think he can be?"

She shrugged.

Birdwing said, "Maybe they all went fishing. The grunion are laying."

"No one asked permisson to go fishing," Father Moreno said. "I have a feeling you are all keeping something from me."

Clarita volunteered: "They are being worked too hard on the rocks."

The priest said, "Oh?" questioningly, surprised.

From Lola, whose conscience must have been pressing her, came "El Loco," spoken softly.

"Yes, yes. What about El Loco?"

"He has been talking against the Fathers in the *rancherias*."

"What has he been saying?" Father Moreno looked from one face to another; and when no one replied he repeated the question, his voice rising: "What has El Loco been saying about us? What lies has he been telling?"

At the end of a prolonged silence, Birdwing said, "When the tide and the moon are right the grunion come in fine. I've seen the beach covered with them when the waves are small and the tide is right."

"I am going to keep all of you here," the padres said, "until you tell me what El Loco has been saying.

Another period of silence ensued, and then the old woman Father Moreno had rescued from being buried alive hesitantly held up her hand.

"Yes, Lolita?"

"He say you bad men. He say you come from bad place. He say Chinigchinich no want you here. He say soldiers take women and do them bad things."

"Well, what do you think? Is there any truth in such nonsense?"

No one moved or spoke. All eyes were cast down.

Father Moreno was incensed. "Some of you don't seem to realize why Father Salvatore and I are here. We are here for your good, for your welfare." His words were bristling with irritation. "We are here in goodness and mercy to teach you and to lead you into the civilized world. Believe me, there are many other things we would rather be doing. We are devoting our lives to making you eligible for the Kingdom of Heaven. If you consider that evil, make the most of it. There are times when my stomach gets sick of the struggle to educate you, and this is one of them. We feed you, we clothe you, we cure your illnesses, and all we ask in return is that you contribute a share of the work which must be done." The priest paused, aware that the tongue-lashing was a waste of breath. No one was looking at him. He continued: "If those men who are missing do not return by vespers, the soldiers will be sent to bring them back. It will go hard with them. Now you may go to breakfast."

Not only did the fugitives not return by sundown, the following morning the remainder of those men who worked at the quarry were missing. "Looks like a conspiracy," Father Moreno said to Father Trujillo, and turning to Sebastian: "Could it be you have been driving them too hard?"

"If you don't keep after them, they do not work at all."

"We've got to get them back," Father Moreno said. "The Mission depends on it."

Ignacio assigned José, Pedro and Vincenti to fetch them.

"Pepito, you'd better go along to interpret. But be careful; look out for treachery."

"Above all, don't trust that El Loco," Father Trujillo said.

CHAPTER SIXTEEN

"I'm surprised we haven't had some word from the posse," Father Trujillo said, coming down a path in the vegetable garden where Father Moreno was weeding. "I thought they'd be back by now."

The senior priest, too, was concerned but he did not think that idle speculation would help any. "Do you know anything more stubborn than dandelions?" he asked.

Father Trujillo said, "Here, let me relieve you," and took the hoe. "Do you think they may have run into trouble?"

Father Moreno, bending over to pull a weed, paused to look up. "Now how am I to answer a question like that? How in Heaven's name would I know whether they've run into trouble or not?"

The younger priest was startled by the sudden irascibility. "Well, I thought—"

"If they've run into trouble we'll hear about it."

Why are you so testy? Father Trujillo wondered. "Suppose they can't find them?" he asked.

"Of course they'll find them."

"Work on the church is at a standstill."

"The life of the Mission itself may be at stake."

As they were speaking Mirabel came tearing down the river trail with Pepito on her back, the boy screaming at the top of his lungs. Both priests paused, harkening, and Father Moreno lifted his skirts and started to run. Falco, dozing at the gate, jumped to his feet, knocking his gun to the ground. He retrieved it, his slow-witted attention riveted on Pepito. Ignacio came out of the guardhouse. The boy slid off Mirabel before she came to a stiff-legged stop. Sides heaving, neck and haunches dark with sweat, she stood legs apart as if to keep from toppling over. "The heathens!—El Loco!—They come!" Blood clotted the boy's face. His shirt was ripped and he looked as if he had been rolled in dirt.

"Who hit you?" Falco asked, the warning not yet having

penetrated his drowsy consciousness.

Without replying, Pepito ran through the gate and, seeing the padres hastening toward him, cried, "The heathens, Father!—they are coming!" Father Moreno caught the boy by his thin shoulders. "El Loco—!" Pepito exclaimed and, flinging himself into the folds of the priest's smelly habit, began crying.

"What about El Loco?"

For moments Pepito was unable to speak. He wept for what he had seen and for the relief he felt at having gained the safety of the Mission. Father Moreno pressed the boy's head against his tumescent belly and they stood thus while Pepito regained his composure. Then, holding the youth at arm's length, the priest demanded, "Tell us what happened."

Pepito related how, when he, José, Pedro and Vincenti had reached the *rancheria* at the hot springs, they had been set upon by a host of natives led by El Loco. The Indians had seized their mounts, had stripped the soldiers of their guns, ammunition and clothing, and had beaten Pedro and José with sticks until they did not move. As for Vincenti, he said they had chased him until he dropped from exhaustion. El Loco had donned Pedro's deerskin tunic and led the mob in a wild dance. Pepito said he had managed to escape when El Loco mounted Mirabel and she threw him; during the ensuing hilarity the boy said he had jumped on Mirabel and she had borne him away in a hail of stones and arrows.

"They say they are going to destroy the Mission and kill you and Father Salvatore," Pepito said, wiping his wet cheeks with the back of a hand. "El Loco, he is leading them."

Father Moreno turned to Ignacio. "We need help. Some one has to go to San Diego for reenforcements."

Ignacio said, "I'll go, Father."

"No. We need you here." He turned to the older soldier. "You go, Falco. Get started right now. And don't spare your horse."

Father Trujillo clanged the bell frantically. Its insistent peals rang out over the countryside, calling the neophytes to chapel. And they came, the old men, the women and the children, some of them running. When all had been accounted for, Father Trujillo and Ignacio swung the gate shut, lifted the bar in place, then jammed a timber against it to make it more secure.

Herded into the chapel, the neophytes sat respectfully while Father Moreno related what had happened at the hot springs. The priest spoke quietly to assuage the congregation's apprehension. "I can't believe your people mean us any harm," he said. "But we must prepare for the worst. If there is an attack you will all come here and stay out of harm's way." He led them in prayer, asking God for protection, then he gave an order to fill every receptacal with water, adding, "The first thing they will do is cut off our water supply."

The hope of defending the Mission lay in the Californians' fear of firearms. For defensive purposes Franciscan missionaries rarely used firearms, and when they did they fired them without shot. Thus it was a surprise to Father Trujillo when Father Moreno asked Falco for a musket loaded with lead.

"You don't mean you would use it?" the younger priest asked.

"I might have to. Christ teaches we are warriors in God's army, Salvatore. If I have to use this gun I shall do so with His guidance. He will not permit these devil-guided heathens to destroy what we've worked so hard to create."

Father Trujillo exclaimed almost triumphantly, "If they kill us, we shall be martyrs!"

Father Moreno sighed, shook his head despairingly and glanced at the women and children filling buckets and baskets with water. He spoke rapidly: "I realize that to you, Salvatore, I am hardly an exemplary priest. And it is true: I break a good many rules. The basic difference in our philosophies, I think, is that you are interested in the glorious hereafter while I am interested in the prosaic present. To me the good one does in this life is more important than that he may hope to do in the unpredictable next. Now let's see to the food supply."

The singing of vespers that evening was lacking in lilt. And after the service the young girls who ordinarily would have been herded into the *monjerio* remained in the chapel with the other neophytes. Children fell asleep, their heads in their mothers' laps.

The faces in the flickering candlelight of the huddled congregation were white-eyed and full of animal apprehension, and running his eyes over them Father Moreno thought: *They are wondering whether they are right, remaining with the foreigners. Would God truly protect them? Wouldn't they be safer with their own people?* The priest wondered if that mysterious, incredibly powerful seed called religious faith, which he and Father Trujillo had so carefully planted in these people, had rooted sufficiently to hold them here. The female, he thought as they sang, is more religious than the male; there seems to be a stronger liaison between her and the Infinite than there is between the Infinite and a male. Perhaps that is because women are the vessels of life, he surmised, the bearers of posterity, a fact which bespeaks a close affinity with the Creator. The connection between God and man can be strong, too, he thought, but incalculably different. Men seem to be the preachers, women the congregation.

Ignacio was stationed as look-out at the main gate, Father Trujillo stayed with the neophytes in the chapel, and Father Moreno, Sebastian and Pepito went to the *cocina*, from which both gates could be observed.

Daylight dissolved without any sign of hostile Californians. Ignacio had built a fire at his post, more for light than heat, and it cast wavey, eerie shadows across the compound. The sounds of insects were the only noises obscuring the nocturnal silence and all seemed peaceful. Nonetheless, in the air there was a portension, an aura of oncoming evil.

"You got the definite impression, Pepito, that they were coming tonight?" Father Moreno asked.

"Oh, yes, Father."

"I'd rather they put it off until daylight. We'd be better able to cope."

Sebastian said, "Iniquity has the advantage in darkness."

The priest said, "Falco should be at San Diego by this time tomorrow. If we can hold out for two days we should be saved."

"Have faith," Sebastian said. "God will not forsake us."

"Yes, have faith," Father Moreno said, "for he who doubts is like a wave of the sea that is driven and tossed by the wind." And addressing Pepito he asked, "Do you recognize that?"

"Yes, Father. It is from the first chapter of James."

"I hope you let it guide your life." And to himself the priest said, *Why don't you practice what you preach? Time and time again throughout your life doubt has crept into your consciousness. . .*

CHAPTER SEVENTEEN

At Falco's strident cry, Father Moreno snatched the candle, spilling hot wax on that hand, and, sheltering the flame with the other, hurried toward the main gate. Pepito and Jesus followed in his wake.

Father Trujillo appeared in the chapel doorway. "Are they coming, Father?"

"They are coming!" Father Moreno cried without breaking stride.

Through chinks in the palisade he saw a broken line of flickering torches. It advanced slowly, ominously like an incandescent snake, and presently, faintly at first, came the sounds of intermittent shouting, sounds which rose and fell, wafted by the wind. Father Moreno held the candle up to Jesus' hirsute face. The latter's dark eyes mirrored the flickering flame. "We can stay and defend the Mission or we can flee," the priest said, asking an opinion.

"Instead of fleeing," the mason replied, "we should go forth to meet them. We are on the side of God. We have nothing to fear."

Father Moreno shook his head as if to clear his ears. "But we are no match for them. There is an unholy mob out there."

"I will go. I am not afraid." Jesus began removing the timber which braced the gate. "God will protect me."

Father Moreno caught his arm. "Don't be a fool! They'll kill you!"

The mason struggled to free his arm. "God sent me to rid the world of sin. This is a fine time to begin."

"The Bible says a prudent man sees danger and hides from it, but the simple go on and suffer for it. Now use your common sense."

"Let me go!" The mason wrested his arm free.

The Priest enclasped him. "Listen to me! Jesus, listen to me! You are not going! I absolutely forbid it!"

The mason wrestled with the priest and in the scuffle the two men stumbled over the bracing timber, toppled it, and themselves tumbled into the dirt. Pepito tried to pull Jesus off the priest, but the former

128

with a kick sent the youth sprawling. Scrambling to his feet, the
mason tried to unbolt the gate, but Father Moreno rose to restrain
him. Violently, fanatically Jesus pushed the priest away and drew the
bolt. The gate began to swing open. Both Pepito and Ignacio threw
themselves against it. The priest again caught the mason's arm and,
shouting his name, shook him trying to penetrate the bewitchment
which had seized him. But the latter was obdurate. He spoke with
great dignity: "Don't forget who I am." And once again he tried to
open the gate, whereupon Father Moreno swung him around and
struck him flush on the chin with a fist.

For a moment it appeared the mason would fall, but he recovered
and putting hands to face burst into tears. The priest used his aching
hand to make the sign of the cross and put an arm around his adver-
sary. "I'm sorry," he said.

"Please let me go," Jesus whimpered. "I can stop them."

"We need you here. We need all the help we can get." The priest
looked through a chink. Falco joined him. "How many are they,
would you say?" the priest asked.

"Hard to say, Father. Two, maybe three hundred."

"Are the guns loaded?"

"They are, Father."

"How many do we have?"

"Six."

"What about the cannon?"

"It's in the guardhouse, Father."

"The guardhouse! What in the name of the Almighty is it doing in
the guardhouse?"

"I don't know, Father."

Father Moreno peered again, said, "They're setting fire to the
grain." A wickiup burst into flame, then another and yet another.
These spark-spewing fires illumed the night and revealed the gleaming, pigment-smeared, naked bodies of the natives. Some were armed
with spears, others with bows or stones and many carried ignited
pineknots. Their shouting had little definition or intelligibility; it was
an uproar rather than a chant and chilling in its wildness. In the corral, the stock, alarmed by the fire and the hullabaloo, added their
fearful voices to the unholy chorus. Pepito asked Father Moreno if he
should open the corral gate and let the animals into the compound.
The priest forbade it, saying, "They'll trample the garden!" A
firebrand came hurtling into the patio and lay burning. Pepito fetched

it and threw it on the fire. Another fell upon the chapel roof. Now arrows, rocks and flaming pineknots came raining into the Mission. One and then another of the thatched roofs caught fire. Father Trujillo led the neophytes out of the chapel and put them to work passing buckets and baskets of water to Pepito who, standing on a ladder, doused the torches as he could. When the roof of the storehouse began burning, Father Moreno boosted Father Trujillo up onto it to put it out. "If that goes we'll all be blown to kingdom come!" he cried, alluding to the gunpowder kept therein. He cautioned the younger priest: "Keep to the edge. The crust is thin." Father Trujillo picked up a torch and flung it over the pallisade at the Californians. "No, no, Salvatore!" Father Moreno shouted. "They'll only throw it back again!"

Thinking that gunfire might frighten the marauders away, Ignacio and Sebastian fired a salvo into the air. The effect was instantaneous. For several moments every voice was stilled and neither a brand nor an arrow fell. Taking advantage of the sudden silence, Father Moreno shouted, "El Loco, are you there?"

"I am here, Father!"

"What are you up to?!"

"We want to come in, Father. We want to be baptized." It was a joke. There was general laughter.

"Laugh if you like," the priest shouted. "This is a sad for your people."

"What you say, Father?"

"I said this is a sad day for your people!"

"Why, Father?"

"God will wreak His vengeance on you."

"You going to open the gate, Father?"

"Not tonight, my son. Come back tomorrow—in peace—and we may let you in."

After a short interval for the Californians to consult, the shouting, hurling and archery were resumed. While Jesus stood urinating on a burning brand, an arrow struck him in the buttock and his bellow momentarily drowned out other sounds. A stone struck Father Moreno on the back and knocked the breath out of him. Now came a rending sound and Father Trujillo disappeared, taking a large portion of the storehouse roof with him. Ensued a frantic rush to assist him. While neophytes helped drag him from the wreckage, Father Moreno and Ignacio removed the pouches of gunpowder. By now several fires were burning within the compound and hundred of embers and sparks were flying through the air in search of tinder. Father Trujillo and the gunpowder were taken to the tiled-roof chapel. Blood oozed from the badly battered priest's forehead.

"Are you all right, Salvatore?" Father Moreno asked anxiously.

Weakly: "I don't know."

"Can you move your fingers?"

Father Trujillo flexed his hands.

"How about your toes?"

Father Moreno helped his brother priest to sit up. While the injured man was moving his arms and legs, testing them, Jesus came running to say that the horde was at the main gate. Father Moreno picked up his gun and cartridge box and went out into the night. El Loco was beating on the gate and shouting to his followers: "Hear my voice, ye warlike birds!—I want the vengeance of your claws!" And the hysterical savages, drunk with evil, screamed their support. Through the chink they could be seen hopping about in imitation of birds. A shaman, wearing a necklace of human fingers, spread hot coals on the ground and, in a hypnotic frenzy, proceeded to walk thereon, his purpose being to cast a spell on the pale men's guns and thereby render them harmless. Others then raked the embers against the gate which quickly flamed.

The several fires made of the scene a netherworld; Father Moreno thought it a miniature portrait of hell. Most of the neophytes within the stockade, uncertain whether to be loyal to the padres or to their own people, skurried into the chapel and huddled there, although a few of the children continued to pass baskets of water to Pepito. When it appeared the gate would soon give way, Father Moreno ordered everyone into the chapel and himself took a position in its doorway.

The marauders, using a battering ram, broke down the burning gate. When the cloud of smoke and dust had dispersed there behind the lickerish flames in the midst of his followers stood El Loco dressed in Pedro's uniform. He was grinning triumphantly. "You no open gate for us, Father," he cried, brandishing a gun, "we open for ourselves!" But for all his bravado, neither he nor any of his followers appeared eager to advance; on the contrary, now that the bulwark had been breached, those in the front rank scrambled to hide behind one another. Whereas moments before, protected by the gate, they had been bloodthirsty warriors bent on mayhem and murder, now they

131

appeared more like timid children. Like children, they tried by grimace and gesture to feign ferocity, but it was obvious they lacked faith in themselves.

Father Moreno called, "El Loco!—I want you to listen to me!" And at the sound of command in his voice the marauders became silent.

El Loco: "I hear you, Father."

"I want you to listen very carefully and understand what I have to say. If you or any one of your friends steps inside this enclosure he will be shot dead. Is that quite clear?" The priest brandished the gun.

El Loco did not reply at once, because those behind him were nudging him forward and he turned to rebuke them.

"Do you understand, El Loco?" Father Moreno shouted.

"It is against the Commandments to kill: is not that what you teach, Father?"

"Heed what I tell you, my son. Take your people and go back whence you came. You've done enough evil for one night."

A whining arrow narrowly missed the priest and bounced off the adobe wall. El Loco managed to say, "Is that the way you say Mass, Father—with a gun?" before the pressure of those behind him forced him to jump over the diminishing flames. The mob surged in after him.

Father Moreno shouted, "Yes, my son!" and indicating the cartridge box: "Here is the chalice! Here—" He raised the carbine to his shoulder, "—is the crucifix! And here is my benediction!" He took aim and pulled the trigger.

A fraction of silence followed the gun's discharge. El Loco seemed to turn as if to retreat, then slumped to the ground. And abruptly the natives, startled out of their insanity, turned and fled pell-mell.

By the time the padres reached El Loco it was too late for extreme unction. Kneeling beside him as his life ran out, Father Moreno offered a prayer: "Oh, Father in Heaven, we humbly beseech You to have mercy on the soul of this poor heathen," the words coming from a dry throat. "And I pray You to have mercy on Your humble servant for having dispatched him. Christ has taught us that one should love his enemy, and loving this man as I did I would not have harmed him had he not been bent on disrupting the work You sent us to do. If my son had acted as he did the result would have been the same. Amen."

They carried the corpse into the chapel and, motivated by that repugnance man has for looking upon the face of death, covered it with a blanket. When the priests came out onto the patio the sprawling light of impervious dawn was clearing the dark hills, and day came surging forth in all its glory to reveal the devastation.

Father Trujillo broke into tears, which prompted Father Moreno to put an arm over his spare shoulders. "Weep not for us, Salvatore; weep for the poor heathens. They are the losers." And though at the moment the senior priest had not much heart in the quotation, he uttered it: " 'Neither shall thou be afraid of destruction when it cometh. At destruction and famine thou shall laugh.' "

Sobbing, Father Trujillo said, "There is no laughter in me."

"Is it not you who is always reminding me that God sends us adversity to test us?"

The younger priest wiped his cheeks with the back of a hand. "And it is true!" he said. "We must not be discouraged."

Their attention was arrested by José who came running into the compound. He had managed to escape by hiding in the brush all night. He reported that Pedro and Vincenti had been beaten to death.

El Loco was buried in hallowed ground outside the Mission. It was a simple ceremony because Californians considered it a mocking of the dead to conduct a burial with chanting, the ringing of bells and other Catholic-Christian customs. No one wept, but two women, appointed to the task by Birdwing who had taken over the office of *alcalde*, alternated at wailing. It was believed that wailing was necessary to get a dead man's spirit on its way to the place where pitahayas ripened the year around. Californians were untroubled by the thought of eternity and seemingly had no interest in the hereafter as Christians envision it. They believed the place where the dead go was four days' journey "beyond the ocean," which is why Birdwing suggested El Loco be buried in a boat. It was an Indian belief that death should be treated in the spirit of the deceased, and at another time, because of El Loco's light-hearted and roguish character, there would have been music, dancing, levity and laughter; but not now, not in this aura of compounded woe.

Feeling that some words were necessary before the corpse was covered, Father Moreno prayed at the graveside for the benighted heathen's soul: "Saint Paul said that on the day he dies, every man's work shall be manifest. 'The fire,' he said, 'shall try every man's work of what sort it is. If a man's work abide, he shall receive a reward. If a man's work burn, he shall suffer loss, but he himself shall be saved'." The priest paused to look at the grim, downcast faces about the grave and wondered whether or not any of them understood. Probably not, he thought, and consoled himself by concluding that the explicit meanings of religious words are secondary to their spirits. "Few if any quit this life in a state of purity and grace," he resumed, "and no one takes with him anything that he owns, neither his beads nor his sins. El Loco's history began supposedly in his mother's womb, but it began a thousand generations earlier than that. To all intents it ends here in this hole. The truth is, only his body has died. His spirit and these expressions of it—his abandon, his exuberance, his good humor and artlessness—these are still with us. His spirit has joined the unseen forces of the world and like a comet it will return again and again. What El Loco was, he is, and what he is, he shall ever be. Amen."

CHAPTER EIGHTEEN

Tortured by his conscience and unable to sleep, Father Moreno was writing in his journal, as usual making tiny letters with his quill to preserve precious paper. The ink was the red juice of a berry the Indians used as a dye. *I am fortunate that the neophytes do not appear to hold it against me that I killed El Loco. In the Californians' code, a man who has killed even his mother and father or committed any other heinous crime, does not lose the esteem of his fellows. Each one does as he pleases, and such crimes as he commits go unpunished unless an offended person, such as a relative, seeks revenge. But have I done the right thing in the eyes of God? Is killing ever justified? . . .*

His quill was interrupted by the arrival of the reenforcements. Consuelo was already at the gate with Ignacio, when Father Moreno reached it, but she remained in the background while the men dismounted. Besides Falco the arrivals numbered eleven, of whom one was an ensign. All were dust-caked and slump-shouldered weary. Falco dismounted and leaned against his horse's flank to keep from falling. The ensign introduced himself to Ignacio and Father Moreno. His name was Joaquin Ramos. Although he must have been aware of her presence, Falco gave Consuelo no sign. He did not want the San Diego soldiers to know that he was married to an Indian.

Ramos was twenty-eight years old, squat, square and muscular. Father Moreno sensed at once that he had a strong liking for authority. Looking at the charred remains of the gate, Ramos said, "I see we're late."

Father Moreno nodded. "They were here last night."

"How many were they?"

"My guess is two hundred."

"Maybe more," Ignacio said.

"We'll rest until daybreak," the ensign said, "then go and teach the dogs a lesson."

While the other moved toward the *cocina* for refreshment, Falco unsaddled his horse and went into his mud house. He had not slept for more than forty-eight hours. Consuelo followed him and helped remove his boots. "You no want to eat?" she asked.

He grunted, "No," and lay back on the bed without making any effort to remove his clothing. She covered him with a blanket and lay down beside him. After a little while, to fill him in on what had transpired, she said, "Father Georgio kill El Loco," but this news brought no comment from her husband. Already he was asleep.

While the soldiers ate, Ignacio briefed them on what had transpired, after which Father Moreno asked Ramos: "How do you propose to punish them?"

"There is only one thing these people respect and that's the gun. We're going to make sure they don't rise again. Next time, padres, you might not be so lucky."

"We must not meet barbarism with barbarism," Father Moreno said. "Kill one innocent person and all will be offended."

The ensign said, "Crimes have been committed, Father. The law says the guilty must be punished."

"That's just the point, sir. How are you going to determine who is guilty and who is not?"

"It was an insurrection. They're all guilty."

Irritated by the soldier's implacability, Father Moreno said, "Now look here, young man. We priests are trying to Christianize these people and bring them into the Church. Any injustice can undermine all we are trying to do."

"I beg you to forgive me, Father," Ramos said, chewing. "You have your job to do and we have ours. Ours is to keep law and order. And with all due respect to you, that we are going to do."

Jesus, who had been sitting in shadow listening, spoke up: "It is written in Matthew: 'Whosoever smite you on thy right cheek, turn to him the other also."

Ensign Ramos chose to ignore the quotation and asked where he and his men could billet. They were directed to the chapel.

When everyone had retired and all was quiet, Jesus took his staff and slipped out into the night. Half a moon and a plethora of stars lightened the darkness. He left the compound by the unguarded back gate and, using the staff as a blind man does to warn him of obstructions, took the path to the hot springs. Hurrying, his eyes straining to pierce the darkness, his ears attuned to hostile sounds, he talked to God: "The world is so full of evil, My Lord, that I wonder even You, with all Your goodness, wisdom and power, can quell it." A stumped toe brought out a curse for which he apologized to God and reprimanded himself. "Christ would not have said that," he muttered. His blood chilled when a disturbed animal scamplered from under his feet. Once he tripped on a root and fell to his knees. But stumbling and praying, he pressed on, bouyed by the belief that what he was doing Christ would have done. "Sacrifice is the secret!" he exclaimed, delighted with himself for having made this discovery and surprised by the loudness of his voice. Even when he turned an ankle and fell down, bruising himself on a stone, his spirits were in no wise depressed. He got up at once and hurried on, unmindful of the pain, happy to be doing God's will.

The ashes of what had been a community fire were still glowing and the acrid odor of smoke hung in the air as he approached the hot springs. A dog barked uncertainly, then another more authoritatively. Others joined in, their chorus sharp with alarm. Jesus shouted the greeting *"Hola!"* trying to get into it a friendly sound. At once there was intense activity. Men armed with bows and spears popped out of hovels and clustered at the fireplace. Fuel was quickly added to the coals and its flares lighted up apprehensive threatening faces.

Advancing into the fire's lambent light, Jesus held out his arms to show that he came in peace. Mixing Chumash and Spanish and gesturing extravagantly, he told the hostile Indians that he had come to warn them that their lives were in danger.

At first the Californians did not comprehend what he was trying to impart and so Jesus with great deliberation repeated what he had said and told his listeners that at daybreak men with guns were coming to punish those who killed the soldiers and burned the Mission. "If they find you here," he said, "they will kill you all. Go into the hills and hide before it is too late!"

He had to repeat this several times before one asked, "How do we know this is not a trick to deceive us?"

"Would I come in the middle of the night to bring you a warning if it was a trick? Do as I tell you. Get away from here as fast as you can."

Another Californian spoke up: "The Mission was put to fire because the priests are trying to make slaves of us. We no have time to fish or dance."

"The padres are trying to save your souls," Jesus said. "They are trying to prevent you from going to hell."

"They tell us hell is a warm place. Might not be so bad."

"These evil men who are coming to kill us," another Indian said, "why does your God not stop them?"

"It is God who sent me to warn you."

"I don't know that I have a soul," one Indian said. "If I lose it I won't miss it." There was general laughter. The natives exchanged words among themselves, whispering for the most part. Then the spokesman said, "We like it here. We can get in the warm water when it is cold."

Another said, "This is our place. This is our home."

And yet another said, "If the soldiers come we will kill them as we killed the others."

"You are no match for them," Jesus said beseechingly. "Their guns will kill you. Their horses will run you down. Go now while you can." And the stonemason's earnestness was such that it touched the Indians' reason.

After another long session with his fellows, the spokesman said they would go. "And you will go with us," he told Jesus. "If the soldiers come to kill us, we will kill you." And even as he spoke two braves caught the mason's arms.

Strong as he was, Jesus was unable to free himself. When he continued to resist, a third Indian began striking him on the back with a stick of wood. "But I have done you a favor!" Jesus cried. "I have saved your lives!"

The fellow who had been wielding the stick said, "We want you to build us a house of stone," calculated to be a humorous remark. It brought general laughter.

Sebastian prayed, "Now, Father, is the time to effect a miracle." Even as this plea went through his mind, dogs began barking. And something came crashing through the darkness from the riverbed.

Believing the soldiers were at hand, the Indians released the hostage and scampered away into the lightening night.

As it happened, the dogs were barking at a bear. The bear went on up the mountain side.

As the soldiers were about to set out the next morning, Father Moreno caught the bridle of Ensign Ramos' horse and looking up at the young officer said, "Be just." At another time he would have added, "my son," but there was a reluctance in him to show the soldier any affection. To Pepito, who was accompanying the posse as guide and translator, the priest said, "I want a full report to send to the

Fater President," hoping thereby to moderate if not stay the executioner's hand.

The soldiers and Pepito set out at a fast trot and had gone hardly a mile when they came upon four natives, three old men and a crippled stripling. As the horsemen approached, the Indians stood aside and waited for them to pass. Ensign Ramos gave the signal to halt and asked Pepito if these were some of the rebels.

"I do not know," Pepito replied. He addressed the Indians: "Where do you come from?"

"From *Pai'yaches*," one of the old men said.

"They're from the lake in the mountains," Pepito told Ramos, then asked the Indian spokesman: "Where are you going?"

"To fish in the great sea."

Addressing Ramos, Pepito said, "I do not think they were among the rebels."

"Well," the ensign said, "they are probably up to some mischief. We'd better put an end to it." And turning to his command, he ordered, "Ready arms!"

"But they may be innocent!" Pepito protested.

"There is no such thing as an innocent heathen," Ramos said and gave the order to fire. The three fell. Ramos then rode over to the bush and shot the man crouching behind it.

"It's unChristian!" Pepito exclaimed. "The padres will report you!"

"Who's in command here, chico—me or the padres?" Then as he and his men reloaded their guns, Ramos said, "We have to teach these people not to kill Spaniards." The ensign heeled his horse, motioned to his men and they rode on. After some hesitation, Pepito followed.

Presently they came upon a lone Indian leading a mule. At sight of the soldiers the man left the mule and, heels flying, took off through the brush. It was but a matter of moments before the posse ran him down. He crouched, cringing with elaborate supplication. "I find horse," he said pleadingly, addressing Pepito. "I take to Mission."

In reply to Pepito's translation, the ensign said, "It is obvious he stole the mule. If he's innocent, why did he try to run away?" Without further ado he raised his gun and shot the man. Whereupon Pepito reined his horse and rode off at full gallop, headed for the Mission.

Leaving the dying Indian, the soldiers proceeded to the *rancheria* at the hot springs, which they found deserted. Systematically they invaded each hut, destroyed everything of value and set fire to what was left, burning to the ground every wickiup in the cluster. They then went on to another *rancheria*, also deserted, farther up the canyon. This, they likewise destroyed.

The troop returned to the Mission toward nightfall and its commander reported that they had not found the bodies of the two missing soldiers. "But you have nothing more to fear," he told Father Moreno. "We have taught the heathen a lesson. They won't give you any more trouble."

"Pepito has told me of your cruelties," the priest said, speaking icily. "Has your education been so limited that you do not know such outrages are profane? Do you think, after what you have done, that we can ever get these people to trust us again?"

"But you killed one yourself, Father."

"With good cause. Kill a man unjustly and you engender hate in all of his kind."

"I'm a soldier, Father, not a philosopher."

"You are a fool," Father Moreno said.

"We had orders to do a job, Father. I'm sorry you do not approve of the way we did it."

"I certainly do not approve of wanton killing. The crimes you have committed are unforgivable."

"I do not expect you, a priest, to see things as I do, Father," the ensign said, adding, "Our job is done. We'll be returning to San Diego."

Ignacio asked, "What about replacement for my two men who have been killed?"

"I will report it to the Commandant," Ramos said.

Father Moreno said, "We need protection. Why can't you leave two of your men temporarily?"

"I have no such authority," Ramos said, and exuding a petulent arrogance he mounted his horse and rode off at the head of his troop.

"*El hiji de la puta,*" Ignacio said softly, which translates into "The son of a bitch." He apologized to the priest.

"My sentiments exactly," Father Moreno said.

CHAPTER NINETEEN

The reprisal outrages so terrified and angered the Californians that for weeks none of those who had run away could be induced to return to the Mission. Those who eventually did return came back because of their wives, and then only after receiving the assurances they would not be punished. *I am distressed by the situation here,* Father Moreno wrote the Father President. *While work on the great church continues, the progress is exceedingly slow. But more important: we are not making conversions. Even the old and the sick distrust us. . .*

Today Inez, obviously pregnant, was washing clothes, humming the while, when Ignacio came into the house and dropped some faggots beside the fireplace. Brushing off his sleeve, he embraced her from behind. She giggled, twisted her buttocks against him, and said, "Wait till I finish."

At this inopportune moment one of the newly arrived replacements, a slight fellow with big ears and buck teeth called Ramondo, came running up to the doorway with the alarming news that a ship was entering San Juan Bay. The immediate assumption was that it was manned by pirates, because some months thereto the Mission Santa Barbara had been plundered by the crew of a privateer.

Ignacio and the other soldiers rounded up the neophytes and herded them into the compound. After a hasty conference, Father Moreno decided to go alone to meet the mariners, refusing both Father Trujillo and Jesus, both of whom wanted to accompany him. "One martyr at a time," he said. "If they kill me you'll get your chance."

Ignacio said he thought at least one soldier should go with him, but Father Moreno said, "If they're bent on plunder, one soldier isn't going to be much help."

About a half mile from the beach the priest saw three fairskinned men coming up the dry riverbed toward him. He shouted to get their attention and hurried on to meet them. All three were gaunt and stubble-bearded. The bow-legged, red-haired one, speaking in broken

Spanish, introduced himself as John Stone, captain of the vessel. He said he and his crew were short on rations and water and that a number were ill with scurvy. "We'll be grateful to trade for whatever supplies you can spare us," he said.

"What nationality are you?"

"English."

"I'm sure you realize, Captain," Father Moreno said, "that it is against the law for us to trade with you or any foreigners."

"Yes, yes, I know." the captain said. "But you are a man of God. I cannot believe you would refuse to help us." Though unspoken, the inference was there: refuse us and we shall take what we need.

"How many are you?"

"Thirty-one."

"What have you to trade?"

"Otter skins."

Father Moreno considered this for a moment before repeating, "Otter skins," and shaking his head. "They are the only things in the world I can think of that we can't use."

"They are very valuable in the marts of Canton."

"For making fur coats. We need none such here."

"You may have anything on the ship, Father. Anything at all. We have some excellent rum. We have tools. I have a spare spyglass. . ."

For one hundred fenegas of grain, four steers and twelve liters of vinegar the religious chose a silver tray for the altar, some pewter mugs, China plates and cups, woolen blankets and a hogshead of rum. Moreover, while the ship remained at anchor in the Bay the ship's carpenter made sturdy tables and four chairs for the padres. Father Trujillo came upon a music box in the captain's quarters and asked Father Moreno if he might trade for it. "I think it will be useful in proselytizing," he said. And to chide his superior he said, "As long as I make no protestation about the rum perhaps you will let me have it."

"But of course, Salvatore. We'll toss in a few more fenegas of grain."

The music box was worked by a crank and the first time Father Trujillo played it in the Mission the neophytes were astounded. Listening to it was the most fascinating entertainment they had ever known and they could not get enough of its magical sounds. Thus confirmed in his opinion, the younger priest one morning packed it on a mule, filled a bag with beads, and announced he was "going fishing. Perhaps this devilish thing will succeed where our persuasion has failed," he said.

Indicating the beads, Father Moreno said, "I see you have become reconciled to bribery," and was pleased when the younger priest grinned.

Leading the mule, Father Trujillo made his way to the sea and followed the coast northward, going into an area neither he nor Father Moreno had explored. After three hours he reached the crest of a knoll overlooking an estuary at the far end of which was a village. As priest and mule approched the settlement a number of the natives fled. Others gathered in a defensive group, the naked men before and the woman and children behind. Their spokesman was a short, thick man whose head was set close to his shoulders. He began his harangue in a dialect unfamiliar to Father Trujillo, but the Indian's gestures made it clear that he and his people were afraid of the mule. The priest tethered the mule to a rock at some distance from the gathering, removed the music box and proceeded to turn the crank. As the first notes wafted through the air the startled natives either fell upon their knees and buried their faces in their hands or ran to their wickiups to hide. But then, as Father Trujillo advanced on them and the music continued, their curiosity overcame their fear and one by one they cautiously clustered about the stranger to listen to his miraculous box.

By the time the machine had run through its repertoire of *Go to the Devil, The Siren's Call,* and *The Hungry Chicken,* every man, woman and child of the village was huddled about the priest and listening with astonishment and delight. Had he understood English, Father Trujillo doubtless would have been appalled by the lyrics. As it was, using sign language he told the heathens the music was the voice of God and then went on to explain that God was the maker of the earth and the sky, the sun and the stars. "He is your father," he told them, mixing Chumash and Spanish with gestures. "And He is building a great house in the south to which you are all invited. To those who come He will give food to eat and blankets to warm, but more important He will give you everlasting life."

This was a little much for the primitive minds to absorb all at once, so the priest repeated it several times. And as an indication of what lay in store for those who accepted the invitation he distributed the beads, explaining they were gifts from God.

The Indians reacted like delighted children. To them the glass beads were precious jewels and Father Trujillo was their legendary god. To show his appreciation, the chief offered the priest his daughter, a rather fat girl in her early teens.

"I am greatly honored," Father Trujillo said. "But does she not have a mate?"

"Oh, yes. She is not a virgin."

"Then it is not right that you give her to another."

"Why not? She is my daughter. I can do with her as I like." The chief made a vulgar gesture. "You are a man, are you not?"

Admitting that he was, indeed, a man, the priest began the difficult task of trying to explain clerical celebacy. But the more he got into the subject, it seems, the less his listeners understood what he was trying to tell them. To them the concept was so unnatural as to be an absurdity.

"Then you are *coia*," the chief concluded, as if that were the only possible explanation.

"No! No!" the priest exclaimed; and with gestures he tried to explain that it was his chioce to eschew all sexual relations. In response the chief dismissed the subject as too complex to understand.

Father Trujillo asked the chief if he might take his daughter and her mate to visit the great church, and the chief indicated with a gesture that it was all right with him. But the girl said she would not go without her mother, and the mother declined in no uncertain terms, saying she was afraid.

The chief said, "Those people to the south do not like us."

Father Trujillo assured the chief that God would protect anyone who came to His house, but the chief appeared unconvinced. Then abruptly, surprisingly, when it appeared that Father Trujillo's journey had been in vain, the chief announced he would go, whereupon his wife, their daughter and her husband said they would go also. Accordingly the next morning, with Father Trujillo playing the music box, they set out for San Simeon.

At the Mission the visitors were accorded every consideration. They were given food and clothing and blankets and adornments, and for their entertainment every evening there were music and dancing. The priests worked hard to win the confidence of the chief, whom they called Toro because of his short neck. Father Moreno told him that all

144

people of whatever tribe were brothers and sisters and should live in peace and harmony, an idea so startling that the priest had to repeat it several times before his listener could grasp it. Father Trujillo persuaded Toro to approach and eventually to mount a mule, and once the Indian had overcome his fear of the creature he became so intrigued that it proved difficult to get him off. Toro was told that if he and his family would come and live at the Mission he could ride a mule or a horse wherever he wanted to go. This offer was powerfully beguiling, but it was not until Ignacio showed the chief that he could kill a rabbit with a gun that Toro became a convert, along with all members of his family.

With Toro in tow, Father Moreno made a second visit to the bay village, taking the music box of course, and they came back to San Simeon with seven more candidates for conversion, four of them females. A third visit netted ten, and a fourth, six. Father Trujillo then took his musical show into the mountains and returned with more adherents.

The people Father Trujillo attracted became in effect his disciples. They held him and his music box in awesome respect and looked to the priest for sustenance and guidance. And the more these people leaned on him, the stronger Father Trujillo became. Through the wonderful alchemy of their devotion and respect he came to find joy in life, in the people and in his work. One day Father Moreno jokingly asked, "Could it be, Salvatore, that I actually heard you laughing?"

"It's possible." The younger priest patted the music box. "This is the best investment we ever made."

Father Trujillo's change in attitude came to have a profound effect on all of the Mission people. Everyone began to take an interest in whatever work he assigned them. And it was heartwarming and a little pathetic to see the pride they revealed at their little achievements. Now there was more camaraderie, more joking and laughter in the Mission, and because of this happy atmosphere all but a few of the natives who had left to join El Loco returned and were granted forgiveness.

As the converts increased, so did God's work. The damaged buildings were reroofed with tile, the main gate was rebuilt stronger than before, and the stockade was reconstructed. Life was coaxed back into the garden. Such grain as had not been burned was harvested and the fields replanted. Meanwhile, work on the great church went on apace and every day the padres preached the virtues.

Today it was Father Moreno: "Take note of the vast and farseeing intelligence which created this world and mankind. That intelligence is God. Male and female made He, as alike as pesos and as different as the coin's two sides. God thought of everything, of every problem and contingency, of the arched foot and the opposed thumb, of the faithful heart and the hateful spleen. He matched despair with hope, ignorance with intelligence. He gave us wills with which to steer our destinies and temptations to lead us astray. He gave us eyes to see others and egos so that we could not see ourselves. He gave us ears to hear, but kept the upper and lower registers for His own communications.

"We have a choice, all of us: purgatory or perpetual life. Only the good will survive, only the repentant will have everlasting life. . ."

By repeating such messages over and over again the missionaries nurtured in the natives the desire to live by the rules of morality, to respect if not love one another and to have faith in God.

One day shortly before Pepito was to leave for Mexico, Father Trujillo said to his superior: "You know, Georgio, when we first came here—or rather after we had been here for a while—I became very discouraged; I all but gave up hope that we would ever be able to make any impression at all on these people. And now look at the miracle that has been wrought. These savages have learned to speak Spanish, and a few have even learned to read it. We have taught them to make and lay brick, to grow food, to weave and to cook and to make tallow. They've ceased killing one another and they no longer live from hand to mouth. Even more important," the younger priest went on, "they have learned the difference between right and wrong, between good and evil. I do believe some of them have even developed consciences. Considering what we had to start with, it truly is a miracle. And you Georgio, deserve the credit. Without your help, your patience and your forebearance it could never have been accomplished."

"We have done it together," Father Moreno said.

"The church will be a monument to your long years of self-sacrifice."

"And to yours, Salvatore."

"When it is finished you will be relieved at last."

"Perhaps. But don't wager on it." Father Moreno sighed. "I've looked forward for so long to going home that it probably will be a disappointment. On the other hand," and he grinned at the thought, "it would be a joy to pass an offering plate and hear the jingle of silver!"

Ignacio and Jesus were eating their noonday meal together under the big sycamore near the church on which they had been working. Despairing of ever being transferred, Ignacio had apprenticed himself to Jesus to prepare himself for employment as a mason once he had returned to civilian life. For months he had been learning the art of cutting, laying and truing stone and had become very good at it. Now his mouth full of *tortilla*, Ignacio suddenly asked, "If you're Christ incarnated, Jesus, why don't you turn this water into wine."

Jesus darted a reproachful look of his apprentice. "Your sarcasm is not appreciated, soldier," he said.

"No, I'm serious," Ignacio said. "You claim to be Jesus Christ. No?"

Jesus almost impreceptibly nodded his head.

"Well, Christ could perform miracles. Rear your ass back and pass me a miracle. Make me some wine."

"I can make wine all right," the mason said. "Don't think I can't."

"All right, do it then. Show me."

"I do it all the time."

"How?"

"By making rain fall on the grapevines."

"Oh, for the sake of Almighty God!" Ignacio said derisively, annoyed at having been made a dupe. "You don't have anything to do with making rain."

"How do you know I don't?"

"All right," Ignacio said, begrudgingly granting a point. "You're Jesus Christ. I want you to do me a *real* favor. I want you to pass a miracle and get me a promotion."

"If you deserve a promotion, you'll get one."

"Aw, come on, Jesus. Quit kidding yourself. You're no more Jesus Christ than I am!"

"Take care, Ignacio. Don't mock God. The day of judgement is coming."

The soldier laughed and said the equivalent of "Horseshit!"

CHAPTER TWENTY

The eve of Pepito's departure for Mexico City to attend the College of San Fernando, Father Moreno took him into his quarters for a farewell. The priest was in a mellow mood, having fortified himself with a few drams of rum. By now Pepito was a handsome youth of sixteen about whom there was an ethereal quality rare in one of his race. In opening the conversation there was a touch of wistfulness in the priest's words: "In all likelihood, my son, this is good-bye. The chances are I won't be here when you return."

The boy did not know what to say. He felt sad.

"I'm proud of you, Pepito. I want you to do well."

"Perhaps on your way home to Spain, Father, you can visit the College."

"Perhaps." And then Father Moreno lightened the mood by speaking of Santa Gertrudis and Pepito's early life. "I chose you from among all of the children because of a quality in you, Pepito. The first time I saw you I thought to myself: that boy has the attributes for priesthood. And I told your mother that you were born to be a priest." He stroked Concha, lying in his lap. Now full grown, she was the only one of the three kittens Ignacio had brought that had survived. Fransquito had been devoured by coyotes and Lola had been killed by a boy with a bow and arrow.

Pepito said, "You have told me, Father, that my mother was a very special person. It pleasures me to hear you speak of her."

"She was very intelligent, and very pretty."

"Why did she die, Father?"

"I never knew. One day she appeared to be well and the next she was dead. It seems that the purpose of her life had been to give you birth." Concha opened her mouth wide, then closed it again, oblivious to what was being said. "I never knew your father," the priest went on. "Your mother told me he disappeared not long after you were born; went hunting for turtles one day and never came

148

back."

"I don't remember him at all."

"Your mother had a delicacy, a grace and gentleness most unusual. She had your skin and your eyes."

The youth was pleased and embarrassed.

Father Moreno reminisced about his own childhood in Spain. A strong influence on his life, he said, had been an old man who sharpened knives and saws for a livelihood. "I used to visit him in his little shop and watch him work," he recalled. "He would tell me stories of the Saints—of Saint Anthony the abbot, who exemplies self-denial; of Saint Augustine, who had such a powerful intellect; of Saint Francis of Assisi, whose great strength was his love for his fellow man; of Saint Ignatius of Loyola, who was the personification of will-power, and of Saint Theresa, the mother, who is the ideal of ecstacy and enthusiasm. These same stories I have told you, Pepito," Father Moreno went on, continuing to stroke the cat. "I learned them from the old knife-sharpener and it was he who first put it in my head that I might have qualifications for the priesthood. My uncle, the Franciscan priest, influenced me, too, but it was the old knife-sharpener who planted the seed. Without his inspiration and kindness I might never have been here, and if I had not been here you probably never would have had an opportunity to become a priest. Thus, you can trace your own destiny back to the old knife-sharpener. That is proof of the continuity of goodness."

"You've always said that goodness never dies."

The priest left off stroking the cat to take a sip of rum. "Likewise, meanness has a way of rebreeding itself."

"Have you ever done anything mean in your life, Father?"

"Oh, when I was a child I was a rascal. I remember when I was six years old I stole some peaches from a neighbor's tree. He complained to my mother and she proceeded to give me a whipping. But her heart was not in it." Father Moreno looked askance at his quest. "Mothers are notoriously bad chastizers," he said parenthetically. "And when instead of crying I laughed, she had to laugh, too. That put an end to the punishment and she never tried to whip me again." The twinkle of humor remained in the priest's eyes. "She used to vow I would end up in the *calabazo*."

Pepito laughed at the absurdity of the notion. "Is it a sin to pick fruit from a tree, Father?"

"It is if the tree belongs to someone else and you do not have permission. It is stealing."

"But how can trees belong to anyone other than God? He makes them; He takes care of them; He produces the fruit."

Father Moreno shook his tonsured head. "Private property," he said. "Everything in civilization is private property—the trees, the flowers, the rocks, everything."

"The land, too?"

"The land, too."

"What about the air and the sky—are they private property?"

The priest nodded. "Owned by the King," he said, and grinned to show he was half-joking.

"Shouldn't the land belong to everyone who lives on the earth?"

"When I say a person owns land," the priest said, "he doesn't really. He only owns the right to occupy it for a while. When he can't use it any more, he either sells or gives the right to someone else."

"I don't think I'm going to like civilization very much, Father."

"Oh, there are many things you will like about it, Pepito. It has many comforts. One can buy almost anything he needs. This man makes shoes, that one makes clothing, another mends clocks and yet another sharpens knives. There is a great deal of running around in circles and unimportant talk, but life in a big city can be exciting." The priest reached for his snuffbox, opened it, took a pinch and sniffed it into first one nostril and then the other.

The youth watched his mentor with an expression of slight distaste. "Do you mean to say, Father, that there is a man who does nothing but repair clocks?"

Father Moreno couldn't speak because a sneeze was growing in him, so he nodded. The sneeze came. Sniffing, the priest said, "And there is a man who does nothing but cry the news."

"The news?"

"The happenings of the day—births and deaths, murders and marriages." Father Moreno grinned at the expression of doubt on the youth's face. "No," he said, "it's true."

"But doesn't everyone know when things like that happen?"

"Not in the cities. Too many people."

"Why do they want to know?"

The priest shrugged. "Man is curious."

"Is the man paid to do this?"

"Oh, every now and then some one tosses him a peseta or two. And if you want him to cry a message especially for you, you pay him

150

for that. It's called advertising."

Pepito shook his head in wonder and nervously cracked his knuckles: a habit recently acquired from Ignacio.

"Oh, you'll find many wonderful things in Mexico City, Pepito." And then suddenly realizing that the conversation had degenerated into small talk, Father Moreno put the cat down and, leaning forward, spoke more gravely. "So now, Pepito, you are off to the big city to become a priest. It is a sacred adventure. You know that the priesthood was founded by Christ to minister to the needs of mankind and that the twelve apostles were the first priests. Upon them Christ conferred the power of ordaining others to carry on the work through succeeding generations. That honor and privilege came to me. Hopefully it will come to you. As a priest you will be Christ's representative on earth, His ambassador of mercy to the sinful, the wayward, the unfortunate and the ill. There is no higher purpose in life."

Came to them the indistinct sounds of singing. Father Trujillo's choir was at practice.

"I pray I shall be worthy," the boy said. "I pray I do not disappoint you, Father."

"I have no fear of that, my son. Just remember that you must accept what the Church teaches. Don't try to rationalize it. Accept the precepts as you accept the miracles of life and death. If the Church teaches what appears to you white is black, then you must accept that it is black. Do you understand?"

The boy nodded. "Yes, Father."

"You've got to believe that Jesus Christ was a man, that he was born of a virgin and that He is the son of God. Have faith that it is so. As Jesus said, if you have faith and tell a mountain to throw itself into the sea, it will happen." The priest tossed off the last of the rum in his cup and stood up. Pepito arose also. They embraced. It was a tender, awkward moment. "Remember, my son, the Ten Commandments are the keys to a good life."

The morning Pepito left was overcast and in the air was the promise of rain. "Even the sky is sad to see you go," Father Moreno said to the boy.

Those gathered at the gate to bid the pilgrim farewell stood watching him pack the saddle of a gray gelding.

"Young Jesus on his way to Jerusalem," Ignacio said childingly. "Mind you don't get crucified along the way."

151

Father Trujillo said, "Shame on you, Ignacio."

Inez was standing, baby in arms, next to her husband. She said, "He no mean harm," taking seriously what was being played in jest. At age sixteen she was in full bloom and her third child was beginning to bulge her.

Stuffing a missal into one of the saddlebags, Pepito said, "You must work on him, Inez. Otherwise he'll corrupt your children."

"Waste of time," Father Moreno said. "He's hopeless."

Inez, aware suddenly that everyone was making light of a sad moment, put her free arm through Ignacio's and leaned against him. "I hope you become a priest, Pepito," she said.

Pepito finished strapping a blanket over the saddlebags and gave a last cinch to the girth. "When I do I'm coming back and save your husband's soul." To show he meant no offense, he offered Ignacio his hand. Ignacio accepted it and they embraced. Pepito said, "For all your sacrilege, 'Nacio, I love you." He then shook hands with Inez, Father Trujillo, Consuelo, Suegra and a number of others before at last embracing Father Moreno.

When the youth was in the saddle, Father Moreno made the sign of the cross. "God bless you, my son."

"Adios, Padre Georgio. Adios, Padre Salvatore. Adios, amigos."

Heeled, the horse set out, moving with considerable dignity, as if realizing he was carrying a future prince of the Church. Trying for humor, Father Moreno called, "When you get discouraged, remember Jonah. He came out all right."

Several children ran alongside the horse for a way, then dropped back and stood shouting, "God bless you, Pepito!"

CHAPTER TWENTY-ONE

Stone by stone the church took form, its progress almost as imperceptible as a man aging. Seventy-five feet long and thirty feet wide, it was flanked by two transepts. The bell tower, forty-five feet high, was visible for miles. The walls were four to six feet thick, the buttresses up to ten feet at the base. The roof was constructed of seven stone domes. Flagstones formed the floor. President Father Serra arranged "through the grace of God and the fellowship of the Holy Ghost" to have a magnificent altarpiece built in Mexico City and shipped in pieces to San Simeon. When put together it was nearly thirty feet high and adorned with numerous cherubs, archangels, lambs, a lion, an ox and an eagle. From its pinnacle the Virgin Mary, holding the child Jesus in one arm, extended the other in welcome. Save for Mary's blue robe and the flesh tones, the entire rococo work was encrusted in a heavy layer of gold leaf. *The gold alone must have cost a King's ransom,* Father Serra wrote Father Moreno, *but gold is necessary to impress the neophytes with the power and glory of God.*

Pepito had been away for almost a year before Father Moreno had a letter from him. It bore good news. Pepito reported that he had been accepted as a candidate for the priesthood. *I am privileged to wear the novice gown of the Franciscan Order, the first Californian to be so honored,* he wrote. *As a postulant, you well know, my hours are filled with prayer and learning, but my meditations are constantly interrupted, I confess, by images of San Simeon and I long for the day I can return to work among the people there. I have not seen much of Mexico City, but that part I have seen is astonishing almost beyond belief. The great cathedral is stupifying. I had thought that the church we are building at San Simeon was the ultimate in size, but the cathedral here is many times larger and its magnificence is dazzling. . .*

Shortly after Inez and Ignacio had passed their fifth wedding anniversary, word came from the Commandant in San Diego that Ignacio was to be transferred to the Presidio of Los Angeles. With the transfer was a promotion to sergeant and a raise in pay equal to one hundred dollars a year. Although Ignacio did not know it, the promotion had come on the recommendation of Father Moreno. Ignacio was delighted not only with the promotion and the raise in salary but because he saw in the transfer a chance to escape his marital responsibilities. While Inez, now eighteen, was still quite pretty, she had a disenchanting proclivity for getting pregnant. Already she and Ignacio had four children and a fifth was on the way. Moreover, Inez had a strong maternal instinct and seemed more concerned with the children than with Ignacio. For him their relationship had lost its excitement, besides which the children got on his nerves.

When he broke the news to Inez, Ignacio pretended the order was against his wishes and said nothing about the promotion or the salary increase. "I'm being sent to some God-forsaken presidio up north," was the way he put it, giving the impression that he regretted having to go. "Chances are there will be a lot of fighting."

"When do we have to go?" Inez asked.

"*We* are not going," he said, emphasizing the word we. "I'm going."

"What do you mean?"

Ignacio assumed an aggressive expression. "I don't even know where I'm going. How can I take you?"

"You mean you're going to leave me and the children?"

Ignacio hedged. "There's no way we can take the children," he said.

"Why not. They're yours."

He was emphatic: "I tell you, I can't take you or the children!"

"But I am your wife! You are my husband!"

"It's impossible. A soldier can't fight with a wife and children tagging along."

Inez's brown face puckered; she covered it with her hands and began to weep. Ignacio embraced her. "It's better for you, Little Rose," he said pleadingly. But when her weeping did not stop he released her, pulled her hands from her face and lifted her chin. She regarded him searchingly through her tears. "You belong here," he said earnestly. "This is your home. These are your people. If I transplant you, you may die." He was surprised how painful the scene was. It was painful because to a degree she was his creation; he had

154

taught her much. But what made leaving her even more painful was the fact that she adored him. "This is not the end of the world," he said. "I'll be back."

"When?"

"I don't know. As soon as I can."

Inez turned from him and ran to Father Moreno. "You told me our marriage was made in Heaven!" she wailed to the priest. "You said it was forever!"

The priest said, "Now calm yourself."

"You told me Jesus was the son of God and that he would take care of me! You told me—"

"I'll have a talk with Ignacio."

"I don't know what to believe!" Inez wailed as the priest turned away.

Father Moreno confronted Ignacio. "What's this nonsense about you not taking Inez with you?" the priest asked.

"If I take her I have to take the children. Is that not so?"

Father Moreno nodded. "Of course."

"That's impossible. The children are too young."

"You mean you don't want to be burdened."

Ignacio shrugged uncomfortably.

"When you were married," the priest went on quickly, "you vowed to cling only unto her, in sickness and in health, until death do you part. Surely, you can't forget that?"

"Now, Father," Ignacio said, trying to sound reasonable. "You married us because you wanted us to produce some children. You wanted to mix the bloods and upgrade the Californians. Well, I've done my part. You wanted children. You've got 'em. They should stay here, and if they stay Inez has to stay."

"She is your wife. If you abandon her you'll be damned as sure as there's a hell."

Ignacio did not want to offend the priest by saying that such fictional prospects left him undisturbed. "Once I get settled," he said, "I'll send for her," there being no resolution in either his heart or his mind to do so.

"For both your sakes, I pray that you do," Father Moreno said, as if he were pronouncing a benediction.

CHAPTER TWENTY-TWO

Father Junipero Serra did not live to see the church at San Simeon completed. He died at Carmel in the year 1784. When news of his death reached San Simeon, Father Moreno wrote at once to Father Firmin Lasuen, who succeeded to the Presidency:

Father Serra's death is a great loss, not only to the California Missions but to all of mankind. Like the Poverello, *he was pure in spirit, pure in heart, loving and gentle in nature, humble in success, patient under persecution, staunch under infirmity, and an inspiration to everyone. We here are selfishly sorry that he will not be present when we dedicate the new church, now nearing completion. Because he worked hard to insure its erection, his heart and soul are in it, and because they are the church is a very special spiritual jewel. Father Trujillo, who designed it, was inspired not only by Father Serra but by God himself. None but God could have guided his hand in carving the decorations which adorn the pilasters, the arches and the dome. Father Trujillo joins me in begging you to honor us with your loving presence upon the occasion of the church's dedication. Knowing how busy you are, we leave the date up to you.*

Now if I may speak of another matter, dear Father President. Some years ago, with Father Serra's intercession, we sent to the College of San Fernando a young California native with the hope that he might become a Franciscan. While we called him Pepe, he has taken the name Juan Baptiste. I am sure you are familiar with his case. He writes that he has taken his vows, and I think it would be appropriate if it could be arranged for him to return to San Simeon for the dedication. Perhaps you will use your considerable influence to effect it. I believe he is the first of his race to become a priest. It occurs to me that, inasmuch as I am retiring, perhaps you will want to assign him here. I have known him since he was a child and feel certain he can be effective working among his own people.

It is to the glory of God that our Mission now numbers more than

700, this despite some contagious fevers which have unhappily taken a substantial toll. One of those who passed away, it sorrows me to report, was our master mason, Jesus Galindo, without whose skilled hands the church could never have been built. His demise came as the result of an accident. While he and two of his helpers were working at the limestone quarry, a landslide all but buried them alive. A great slab of stone smashed one of Jesus' legs, badly lacerating it.

Father Moreno resumed writing: Jesus Galindo was a devout Christian and an admirable man in every respect. He believed himself to be Christ reincarned. I assumed this was self-delusion, but he earned our respect and admiration by his sterling character and by his deeds. He was the most prodigious worker I have ever known. Absolutely tireless. And without his knowledge, his dedication and his zeal the church still would be but a dream. I am certain Galido was no more the son of God than the next man, and yet he was a very unusual person, one whose life was dedicated to Christian principles. So perhaps he was.

Due to the unusually long spell of dry weather, crops this year have been scanty. We have gleaned so far but 1,500 bushels of wheat, 300 bushels of barley, 400 bushels of corn, 300 bushels of beans, and 150 bushels of peas, lentils and garbanzos—hardly enough to see us through the winter. However, the orchards have been rewarding and we have obtained a fine harvest of olives from which we have extracted a good supply of oil. We have also pressed in excess of 400 gallons of excellent wine, which we are eager to have you sample. Our new tannery is in operation and we are making sandals, saddles, belts and other useful articles of leather. And our weavers are producing cloth for clothing and blankets. Thus we have made good progress despite the drought.

Recently a ship flying the flag of the new United States of America, the frigate Liberty, Everett Sloan master, anchored offshore and we sold Mr. Sloan 400 cattle hides for 20 reales each, so we have some cash with which to purchase things we need for the new church. One thing we need is a proper bell to grace the beautiful belltower. I have ordered one from the supply depot in Loreto and we hope to have it installed for your loving hands to ring at the dedication. We await with eager anticipation word when you can join us for that great and glorious occasion. . .

The bell for the new church came to San Simeon on the same ship which brought Pepito. Indeed, as the vessel bore down on that great arm of land which fists out into the sea to form San Juan Bay, the young priest, attired in the gray habit of a Franciscan, was sitting on it. Its rim had a diameter of thirty inches and its clapper weighed more than twenty pounds. Lashed to the deck, it was sure protection against shipwreck.

It had been seven years since Pepito departed this tiny toehold of civilization, and now as the *San Carlos* moved slowly toward the shore there was much eagerness and impatience in him. His olive-black eyes hungered for familiar scenes and faces. He was particularly eager to greet Father Moreno, to demonstrate his gratitude and affection, and to bask in his mentor's approbation. At sight of the imposing *campanario* rising sharp and clear against the graceful, treeless hills he remembered so well, nostalgia welled in him and he felt such a spiritual ecstacy, such joy and gratitude that he knelt and, hands clasped on the bell, thanked God for having brought him safely home.

As more and more of the Mission hove into view the magic of his mind flipped the years to the time he had burned down the granary. He had gone thither with a lighted candle to fetch some wheat and, finding several bats flying about, had set the candle down to chase them out. In flailing at them he had knocked over the candle, it had ignited some straw, and, presto, the entire place was in flame. Save for scorched feet, suffered in trying to stamp out the fire, he had escaped injury; but much damage had been done and Father Trujillo had wept. Pepito remembered vividly Father Trujillo weeping, because thereto he had believed that priests were not susceptible to weaknesses. With the help of God the fire had been extinguished before it could spread to adjacent buildings. And Pepito recalled how surprised he had been not to be punished. Father Moreno had passed the incident off as "an accident." Pepito thought of Father Trujillo, of his fretful fussiness, remembered his headlong haste, his rigidity, and the fervent way he used to pound his chest with a stone when he preached. Their relationship never had been close and Pepito wondered whether or not Father Trujillo would accept him as a brother in Christ.

Some time before the *San Carlos* hove to, Pepito saw through the Captain's spyglass the welcoming party hurrying toward the beach. And by the time the crew had lowered a boat dozens of people had gathered there. Father Moreno, skirt tucked into his waistcord, came out into the water to help beach the boat which brought Pepito, and Pepito thought how much older he looked than he had remembered him. On the sand the two men embraced. "It is really you, my son!"

As for Pepito, he was too full of emotion to speak; he clung to his mentor for a long moment without saying anything. Meanwhile the natives crowded about them eager to have a close look at and to touch this man of God who was, like them, a Californian. Presently Father Moreno held his protege at arm's length and looked into his countenance; in his moist gaze were mingled pride, admiration and affection. "Why, I believe you've grown a foot!" he exclaimed. "You're almost as tall as I am!" Father Moreno turned to greet the ship's captain, and the awed Californians closed in on Pepito, jabbering questions. To them it was something of a miracle that one of their own kind had become a priest. Rather than try to reply to individuals, Pepito addressed the group, speaking Spanish, saying how happy he was to be home. While he was doing so Inez pushed her way to him and began tugging at his habit.

"Pepito!" she cried, her round face radiant with excitement. Pepito noted that she was even more beautiful than he remembered. "It's me," she said. "Inez."

"Inez!" he exclaimed joyfully, genuinely happy to see her. He took her small hands in his own and stood back as well as he could to look at her. She had taken pains to make herself attractive. Several strings of beads hung from her neck and she had applied pigments to her hair.

"You have become such an important man," she said, "I thought you might have forgotten me."

"Of course not." He looked around. "Where is Ignacio?"

"Ignacio?—Oh," she said, feigning indifference, "he left long ago. He was transferred to the *Presidio de Los Angeles*."

"You didn't go with him?"

Inez laughed too loudly, trying to hide the wound. "He is a soldier," she said indifferently, as if that explained everything. By now Consuelo was tugging at his sleeve, trying to call his attention to her daughter, Maria Magdelena. Maria was twelve and nature was beginning to endow her with alluring and seductive attributes, with witchery and temptation. She reminded Pepito of Inez at that age, and he said as much to Inez, but his words were lost in the conflict of sounds. Seeing Father Trujillo, Pepito pushed his way to him.

"Welcome home!" Father Trujillo said, and, to the younger

man's surprise, embraced him. "Congratulations on your tonsure."

Pepito removed his wide-brimmed black hat and rubbed his head. "Since I have been on this journey, it has almost grown out," he said. "I am badly in need of a haircut."

Father Moreno came up and said, "Come, let us show the captain and our new brother the church," and took Pepito by an arm. With the priests and the captain leading the way, with dogs and children running and yapping and yelling alongside, the throng moved off toward the Mission.

Pepito said, "You are still here, Father."

"I am just before leaving," Father Moreno said. "Now that you are here, I can go."

"It is time. You have given your life to this place."

"It has been a rewarding experience."

"The church, I am eager to see it," Pepito said. And then after a slight pause: "Inez tells me Ignacio has been transferred. Why didn't she go with him?"

"He promised to send for her." Father Moreno gestured hopelessly. "It has been more than two years now." He indicated one of the boys running alongside them. "That's her eldest child. Lucas his name is. There are five." The boy referred to had a fine, light-complexioned, laughing face. "In some ways he reminds me of you at his age." The priest chuckled adding, "He's always up to some mischief."

The church reflected the sweat and blood, fury and love, pain and patience, wish and will which had gone into its construction. Designwise it had something of the artlessness of a child's drawing: slightly out of kilter here, a little lopsided there; and no two of the four arches which connected it with the chapel had turned out to be of the same width, as intended. But in some artful way, these defects, far from detracting, served to give the ediface a certain charm; and despite the miscalculations which had gone into it, it had grace and was in a homemade way even beautiful. Curlicued and keystoned, arched and buttressed, windowed and doored, niched and altared, staired and balconied, roofed and floored, the mass of stone and mortar exuded the spirituality, sublimity, sanctity and holiness that penetrated deep into one's consciousness. It was a magnificent testimonial to faith and the human spirit, and it had the uncanny power of art to pull at the heart.

The architect who had been largely responsible for its creation

160

could not entirely hide his pride in the ediface. "It may not compare with the Cathedrals in Mexico and Madrid," Father Trujillo said to Pepito, "but we believe it is the finest in California."

"Whatever its faults," Father Moreno said, "of this we can be sure: no one can burn it down."

Inside, the church was cool as Heaven must be cool, and there was a majesty about the great vaulted expanse which held out the sky. Entering it, one was moved to silence, as one would be entering the presence of the Almighty. Doorposts and lintels were decorated with paints and carving in native designs—scrolls, serpents and swastikas. There were religious images in some of the niches and a crudely painted banner depicting Jesus on the cross hung from a wall.

"I'm afraid the heathen rather than the Christian influence prevails in the decorations," Father Moreno apologized, "but we wanted to preserve the native culture."

In the afternoon Father Moreno officiated at a Holy Mass to celebrate Pepito's homecoming and Pepito assisted him in it. The young priest spoke the Latin words with good accent and enunciation, better even than Father Moreno, and the latter could not refrain from smiling with satisfaction at the memory of Pepito as a child stumbling over them.

After the Mass Inez came to Pepito and asked if she might see him alone. They went into the sacristy. "What am I to call you now?" she asked.

"I have taken the name Juan Baptiste." He felt uncomfortable with her, as if she were a temptation.

"Should I call you Father?"

He shrugged. "It is appropriate."

"You're still Pepito to me," she said.

He smiled. "There is no more Pepito. When I became a priest I gave up my past."

"How can you give up your past?"

"It wasn't easy," he said wryly.

"Now that you're a priest, can you confess me?"

Pepito responded hesitantly: "Why, yes—of course."

She took his hand and led the way to the confessional.

"Wouldn't you prefer Father Georgio or Father Salvatore?"

"No, I want you to hear it," she said.

"Very well." He stepped into the booth, closed the blue velvet curtain Father Morena's sister Josfina had sent from Spain, and sat down. Inez knelt at the aperture.

Pepito began praying: "Oh, Almighty and most merciful God, Your child Inez, who has sinned, prostrates herself at Thy feet to implore Thy forgiveness. She desires now to comply with Thy holy institution of the Sacrament of Penance. She desires to confess her sins with all sincerity to Thee and to Thy minister. Please, dear God, hear her." He then spoke to Inez: "Repent and thy sins will be forgiven thee."

"I have lustful thoughts, Father."

"Then put them out."

"I cannot. They will not go. They're about you, Pepito."

For a moment the young priest was too surprised and embarrassed to speak; then, speaking rapidly as if delay was dangerous, he said, "It is not important who they are about. You must expunge them at once."

"Remember how we used to play together," Inez asked plaintively.

"We were children."

"I loved you, Pepito."

"Inez, you must call me by my religious name. I am a priest now, and even if you don't respect me, you must respect what I stand for."

"I will always love you." Her whisper had become husky.

"That is over, Inez. You must forget it. I have taken the vows of a priest. I cannot return your love."

"I thought priests were supposed to love everybody."

"And so they do."

"Then why can't you love me?"

"You want a physical love. This I cannot give."

"You used to lust for me. You can't deny it."

"That was long ago. I do not lust for you now."

"Who will know?" she whispered huskily.

"*I* will know. Now stop this nonsense. You will say one hundred Hail Marys and you will ask God every hour to help you put these evil thoughts out of your mind. Do you understand?"

"Please kiss me," she said, her forehead pressed against the top of the aperture, her lips pursed. "*Por favor—*"

"Stop making a fool of yourself," he said sharply. "Repeat after me. Oh, my God—"

"Oh, my God—"

"I am most heartily sorry for all my sins—"

162

"I am most heartily sorry for all my sins—"

"I detest them above all things because they displease Thee—"

Suddenly Inez put her face in her hands, burst into tears, got to her feet and fled.

CHAPTER TWENTY-THREE

Because the swelling waves which burst upon the beach that day sometimes attained a height of ten feet, getting the precious bell ashore posed a problem. If in the process it was dumped into the sea there was little chance it could be retrieved. To prevent this, two skiffs were planked together to carry it, and four oarsmen, for the balance as well as thrust, were assigned to row it to shore. For a time the oarsmen held the clumsy craft beyond the breakers awaiting one of the lesser swells; and, once committed, they rowed hard to catch the crest. For a horrible moment it appeared that the overloaded catamaran was doomed. It swung broadside to the oncoming wave and seemed almost certain to overturn. But something of a small miracle occurred: as if guided by the hand of God, the breaker passed under it and the makeshift craft swung around and glided stern first onto the beach. At once the three priests converged upon it.

When he read the inscription etched in the metal—AVE MARIA PURISIMA, RUELAS ME HECHE, ME LLAMA SALVATORE, 1760—Father Trujillo exclaimed. "Look!—it is my bell!—See, my name is on it!"

He explained his elation by saying he had lived near the Ruelas foundry in Campagna at the time the bell had been cast and had contributed to its fabrication. "When I was six years old," he told his companions, "a man asked me to shine his boots, and for this service he gave me a *real*. It was the first money I had ever owned.

"All I knew about money was that it was a magical substance which could be exchanged for candy and fruit, so I started at once for a sweets shop. Passing the Ruelas foundry I saw a number of people gathered in some sort of ceremony. Being curious, I squirmed my way to the front rank. What I saw was a great cauldron of bubbling, molten liquid which cast a pink glow over the faces of the men stirring it. I asked a nun what the men were doing." Father Trujillo continued, "and she told me they were about to cast a bell, one she said

164

whose voice would carry the message of God throughout the world. Even as she spoke, the famous bell founder, Paula Ruelas, stepped forward to say that the time had come to 'sweeten the voice' of the bell. He explained that a bell's tone is improved by the addition of silver to the mixture of copper and tin. 'Is there anyone present who would make a silver offering?' he asked. A gaudily dressed woman removed a bracelet and tossed it into the pot. Others added silver coins. These gestures of sacrifice generated a wonderfully uplifting emotion," Father Trujillo went on, speaking rapidly and fervently, "and I was caught up in it. The *real de plata* in my fist began to burn. I was faced with a monumental decision. Would it be selfishness or sacrifice? Although I did not realize it then, that was a very important moment in my life. The decision I was to make, I think, determined the course of my life. I was tortuously torn. But even at that age I must have realized the moral difference between the choices, for, after anguished hesitation, I pitched the piece of silver into the steaming mixture. That simple act determined my destiny. At once I experienced a profound feeling of elation, one which reached deep into my soul. Had I spent the money selfishly, I probably never would have become a priest. I probably would have become rich instead," he added, smiling faintly to emphasize the jest. "As the coin sank into the molten metal there appeared a tiny bubble which soon burst. There went my sweets. Almost at once the officiating priest came over and put a hand on my head. To this day I remember the comforting feel of his hand, its approbation and affection. He said, 'Bless you, my son. The Lord has witnessed what you have done.' He asked me my name and, when I told him, said, 'Very well, Salvatore, the bell shall bear your name and it will be bound spiritually to you forever'."

Thereafter, Father Trujillo continued, he went daily to the foundry to watch the bellmakers trim "his" bell, an exacting operation to find its true tone. With each cutting the tone grew sweeter, he said, until at last Senor Ruelas had declared it perfect.

"Now, after more than thirty years, God has sent my bell to me," he exulted. "That we meet again here on the other side of the world is nothing less than a Divine miracle! It means that we shall have a happy church!"

And in Father Trujillo there was such jubilation that it infected his listeners and lifted up their spirits. Father Moreno shouted, "Let us pray," and everyone on the beach got down on his knees, bowed his head and listened to the prayer of appreciation. When God had been duly thanked for this precious manifestation of His love, Father Trujillo blessed the bell by intoning the prayers of exorcism and by washing it with consecrated water scooped from the sea. He then dried it with a cloth, breathed upon it to signify the expulsion of the Devil and annointed it with oil to symbolize the gift of the Holy Spirit. "Here," he said, indicating the bell, "is proof of the trust of that the passage in Ecclesiastes: 'Cast thy bread upon the waters, for thou shall find it after many days'. No investment could have brought me more happiness. Indeed, I am so happy I am ashamed."

Everyone wanted to have a hand in pulling the cart which carried the bell to the Mission, and they went grunting, joking and laughing, now one helping, then another. Once they had gotten it inside the church there was the task of raising it by means of a block and tackle to its proper place in the campanile. Fastened there with anchor chain, the moment came to hear its voice toll the Angelus. With great joy, Father Trujillo seized the bellrope and tugged, and the sweet, clear, reassuring voice of the bell went ringing out over the valleys and hills, its reverberations diminishing as they carried their tidings into eternity. "Come, come into my arms," it sang. "Come find love and be cleansed and reborn. . ."

Among the missionaries who came to attend the dedication of the new church was one from Mission San Gabriel de Archangel, near the Pueblo of Los Angeles, and accompanying him as his military escort was Ignacio. When they arrived, Inez was in the church polishing the altar silver in preparation for the celebration. Consuelo ran to tell her. Inez appeared unmoved by the news. Instead of rushing to confront her husband, as one might have thought she would, she calmly went on with her work.

"Aren't you going to come welcome him?" Consuelo asked.

"If he wants to see me he'll find me,'' Inez said.

Even as she was speaking, Igancio appeared in the church doorway and sang out: "Inez! Look who's here!" He advanced down the aisle in high good humor, a soldier returned from a war. "Did you think I wasn't coming back?"

Inez, polishing a monstrance, did not look up and did not respond. Consuelo thought it prudent to withdraw and did so.

Approaching Inez, Ignacio asked, "What's the matter? Aren't you glad to see me?"

Still she did not speak or so much as look at him. He was even more astonished, when he moved to embrace her, that she shrank away. "Leave me alone," she said.

"What do you mean, 'Leave me alone?' You're my wife."

"I was your wife. I don't need you any more." She stiffened when he embraced her.

"What kind of a welcome is this?—Your long lost husband comes home and you give him the cold shoulder."

"Let me go!" she snarled and, with the fury of a wronged female, wrenched herself free.

"Well, I'm damned!" he exclaimed. Being snubbed by a female was a new and demaning experience for him. After an indecisive moment he said, "Where're my children? They'll be glad to see me."

"They don't need you either."

"I came to take you back with me," he said. "But if this is the way you're going to act, I'll be damned if I will."

Inez said nothing, although her attitude seemed to soften somewhat.

He released her, shrugged, pretending the grapes were sour, and turned to go. "Well, that's that."

As he moved away she said softly, "You waited too long."

He spun back to face her. "I told you I'd come back when I could! This is the first chance I've had! And I wangled this assignment so I could come get you and the children. I shouldn't have left you in the first place. I've come to realize that you are more important to me than anything."

Inez looked at him steadily for a long moment. "Do you mean that, Ignacio?"

"Of course I mean it."

"What you're saying is you truly love me?"

He nodded. "That's right."

"And you want to take me and the children back with you?"

"That was my intention."

She put down the monstrance, said, "Oh, 'Nacio," and embraced him.

While they were in bed together he told Inez that he was going to apply for a land grant so that when he was mustered out he could become a *gente*, a *don*. He did not say that the grant would be denied him unless the application bore his wife's signature.

167

The morning of the dedication the music of the new bell awakened Father Moreno and for some unaccountable reason he felt depressed. He had spent the night in the storeroom, having given up his chamber to the Governor of Upper California, Don Jose de Arrillaga. Indeed, every room in the Mission had been vacated by its habitual occupant to accomodate a visiting dignitary. As was his wont, the priest went to the door and, gazing into the void of cloudless sky, said, "Good morning, God," but today his greeting did not contain his usual cheerfulness. *What's the matter with you?* he asked himself. *Why are you so irritable? This is a day to rejoice.* At times he had known his humor to be affected by an aching tooth or rheumatic joint, but today his peevishness seemed more mental than physical. Perhaps it was the exceptionally dry weather, he thought, and proceeded to say his office by rote, unable to muster much enthuisiasm for it. Crossing the patio to the kitchen, he spoke to old Birdwing, sitting on a bench beside the whitewashed wall. *"Buenas dias,* 'Wingo."

Birdwing's shock of white hair contrasted with his leather-brown face. *"Dias,* Padre."

"Going to be a hot one," the priest said, and went inside.

Already two girls were at work preparing breakfast for the distinguished visitors. They had unbanked the fire and were mixing batter for pancakes. The priest checked the dining arrangements, took a whiff of the steaming chocolate and, finding the orange basket empty, handed it to the one of the girls to refill, adding a complaint that he had to watch every detail. When he left the kitchen, Birdwing said, "I don't like it, Father," looking up at the cloudless sky.

The priest paused and asked vexedly: "What don't you like?"

"The weather. It's too dry and still. It bodes evil."

"Nonsense." Father Moreno picked up a broom and saying, "Here, make yourself useful," handed it to him. "There'll be no breakfast until after Mass."

Governor Don Jose emerged from Father Moreno's chamber resplendent in a bemedaled uniform. He greeted the priest pleasantly. Two of his front teeth were missing and their absence gave him an idiotic look.

Feigning cheerfulness, Father Moreno asked if he had rested well.

"Indeed, yes, Father. I always sleep well when I have had a sufficiency of good wine. And yours is excellent, almost as good as we have at home."

Father Moreno said, "It's going to be a scorcher," and suggested the Governor might like to remove his jacket until the festivities begin. The Governor declined, saying he was quite comfortable whereas, in truth, he did not want to lose his imposing dignity.

"It's been a year for buzzards," Father Moreno said. "We haven't had any rain since I can remember. There's hardly enough water for baptisms."

The Governor said, "Soon you won't have that problem. You'll be in Spain."

"I'll still worry about my children here."

"They'll miss you."

Father Moreno smiled wryly and shook his head. "Not the Californians. Sentiment is not one of their virtues."

"Surely they are aware of the sacrifices you have made for them."

"It is not the Californian's character to be grateful," the priest said. "Instead of looking upon that which is given him, he beholds only that which is withheld. When I leave, it is I who will weep."

"Where in Spain will you go?"

"To Malaga. And the first thing I will do after thanking God for seeing me safely home is to go to a concert. I hope they will play many violins. And I would like to drink *amontillado* from a crystal glass and bathe in fresh, warm water with pure soap in a marble tub and dry myself with fresh linen—all worldly, selfish, unpriestly desires."

By now others were appearing, among them the Father President of the Missions, Estevan Tapis, who recently had succeeded Father Lasuen. He was attired in the trappings of his office over a voluminous red robe and carried an aspergillium. Father Moreno greeted him and said, "Just a few minutes, Father, and we'll be ready." Pepito was lining the Indians against the palisade. There were a great many of them. It seemed that every man, woman and child within sound of the bell had come for the ceremony. Father Moreno went over to give him instructions. "You may let them go in now," he told him, "but keep the center aisle free until Father Tapis and the other visitors have passed." Then as the Indians began filing into the church, Father Moreno returned to Father Tapis and said to him: "In your prayers, Father, I urge you to include a plea to our Heavenly Father to spare us a few drops of rain. We are parched. Only a trickle comes from the spring and there is no grass for the animals."

"Of course," Father Tapis said. "We shall have a mass prayer for rain."

Father Moreno looked up at the cerulean sky. "We've been

imploring Him for weeks, but apparently our voices are not loud enough to be heard; either that, or the Devil has intercepted our prayers. Perhaps you can get through to Him. We have become so desperate for water that last week we resorted to superstition. The Indians claim that strangling two hawks never fails to bring rain, so we strangled two hawks." Father Moreno gestured hopelessly. "You see what good it has done. The shaman says we erred by not strangling them under a full moon. Superstitious nonsense!"

A procession was formed, with Father Tapis at its head. He was followed by the other religious, by the Governor and the military, and, finally, by the *gentes de razon*. Thrice these colorfully costumed people paraded solemnly around the church, once for the Father, once for the Son and once for the Holy Ghost. Father Tapis sprinkled holy water as he went, and each time he passed the front entrace he tapped the great door with his aspergillum, the while intoning, *"Terribilis est locus iste: hic domus Dei est, et porta coeli et vocabitur alua Dei."* The other religious responded, "Alleluia! Alleluia!"

Thereafter, while those Californians who had not been able to get inside the church watched slack-mouthed, the Father President strewed the ground in front of the church with ashes. In these, Father Moreno, using a crosier, scratched the Greek and Latin alphabets, symbols designed to transform the stone ediface into a tabernacle of God.

Sunlight beaming through the high windows to the east highlighted the gold and silver embroidery of Father Tapis' splendid chasuble as he entered the church. Coincidently two young Indian acolytes, coached and cued by Pepito, entered the church by the sacristy door and lighted the altar candles. As the wicks flickered into glow their light was reflected in two gold-framed mirrors hanging on either side of the altar, so placed that priests while celebrating the Mass might observe the congregation. With the brightening light the nine statues in the niches of the reredos appeared to step from their shadowed recesses. Pictures depicting the fourteen stations of the cross hung from the stone walls, as did a banner bearing on one side a scene from the life of the Virgin and on the other Satan roasting in flames.

The Indians, although accustomed to Catholic pageantry, were awed by the splendor, the pomp and the ceremony. Those able to enter the church dutifully genuflected, crossed themselves and knelt to pray, as they had been taught. In the choirloft above the entryway the musicians and singers, under the direction of Father Trujillo, prepared for their parts in the service; and with the beginning of the Introit the neophyte orchestra of flute, gourds, drums and shells added a sweetness to the untrained voices.

Father Tapis, assisted by Fathers Moreno and Pepito, went through the ceremony of the Mass, speaking of course in Latin, a language incomprehensible to the natives. Communion was prolonged because of the number to be served. Before performing the Last Gospel, the Father President climbed to the hanging pulpit, of which Father Trujillo was so proud, to speak Spanish words appropriate to the occasion. For a few moments he stood in silence, looking benignly down upon the colorful congregation, affording everyone an opportunity to feel the strong spirituality which pervaded the church.

"Behold!" he began, extending his draped arms in an all-embracing gesture. "Behold, what man has wrought from the common ground, with only his mind and his hands and the help and guidance of Almighty God!"

Those outside, eager to hear words they could understand, pressed to get inside. A disturbance at the entrance ensued and Father Moreno, seated on the dais, moved to quell it. As he stepped down into the center aisle he sensed what he thought was a slight tremor and for a moment hesitated, stayed by apprehension; but inasmuch as there was no sign of panic he decided he had been mistaken and moved on down the aisle.

"Into this magnificent temple," Father Tapis continued, speaking in a strong, oratorical way, "God has put His measureless spirit and infinite love. This church is His house. It is a miracle of toil, patience and ingenuity. It is a sanctuary for the weak, the afflicted, the weary and the troubled. It is a monument to man's dependency on God. And it stands foursquare, radiant and glorious, against the Devil, his skepticism and his mockery. . ."

Father Moreno had not reached the crowded entryway when, with bloodchilling suddenness, an horrendous quaking of the earth wrenched the church. Instantly the congregation exploded into panic. Everyone scrambled frantically to get outside. Terror precluded reason, and Father Moreno was caught up in the fearful frenzy. The slight, the weak and the aged had little chance; they were knocked down and trampled. The commanding cries of the priests went unheard. While screaming people fought to get out of the jammed doorways a low-pitched rumble issued from the earth and was followed by a tremblor of such magnitude that Father Trujillo's bell clanged. The campanario cracked with a rending sound and pieces of it, together with the precious bell, came crashing onto the roof of the choirloft. The bell plunged through it, barely missing Father Trujillo by inches and crushing to death two of the musicians. Another quake split asunder the center dome and its stones rained down, smashing to the floor a number of those struggling in the center aisle. Father Moreno was among them.

Fragments of roof were still falling when Pepito reached his stricken mentor and began frantically removing the heavy stones which partially covered him. Blood was spurting from Father Moreno's head. While trying to stop the flow, Pepito asked Mary, Mother of Jesus, what was happening. "Don't let this good man die!" he prayed, and began the plenary indulgence proper to the Order of Saint Francis. Other missionaries were trying to bring some order out of the chaos or tending the injured and dying. Presently Father Moreno's eyelids fluttered. He moved an arm. "Father!—Father Georgio!" Pepito exclaimed, speaking prayerfully. "Are you all right?"

The stricken man opened his eyes. His words came slowly: "Pepito, is that you?"

"I am here, Father. There was an earthquake. The roof fell in." Pepito turned to seek help. *I should get him outside*, he said to himself. He tried to lift the wounded priest's shoulders. "Can you sit up, Father?"

Father Moreno tried weakly to rise. He lay back with a sigh of exhaustion. "I guess I can't. I don't seem able to move my legs." Endeavoring to do so, he grimaced, asking, "Is everyone else all right?" His eyes gazed unfocused at the ruptured roof and the blue sky. The wails of the wounded answered him.

Pepito said, "Don't worry about others. We have to think of you."

"Don't bother with me, Pepito. I'll be all right." And closing his eyes, Father Moreno asked, "Is the church badly damaged?"

"I've got to get you out of here."

"I can see the sky," Father Moreno said without opening his eyes. He spoke vaguely, as if he were not certain as to his whereabouts. "I can't move my legs," he said again, and opened his eyes. Tears were running down Pepito's cheeks. "Oh, my son, do not weep." A stone fell nearby.

Pepito arose and cried frantically: "Won't someone help me?"

but his words were lost in the other noises.

"Pepito—"

"Yes, Father."

"Why are the bells ringing?"

"There are no bells ringing, Father," Pepito replied, and immediately regretted having said it.

The stricken priest patted the young man's knee. "How is Father Tapis?"

"He's not hurt."

"How about Father Salvatore?"

"I don't know, Father."

"Pepito, I want you to listen to me."

Pepito leaned closer. "Yes, Father?"

"Don't take the dogma too seriously. There is a lot of nonsense about religion." Father Moreno's eyes were closed and he was speaking with obvious difficulty. "Use your common sense. Don't be too rigid."

"Oh, Father Georgio, you sound as if you were going to die! You're going to be all right! Remember, you're going home to Spain!"

The stricken man smiled weakly. "Going home."

Pepito saw Father Trujillo dispensing water to the wounded. By now save for the priests, the wounded and the dead, the church was empty. Pepito stood, called and waved and Father Trujillo came quickly with the water. Pepito lifted Father Moreno's head and asked him to open his mouth. Some of the water ran down the stricken man's bloodsmeared chin. Pepito wet the skirt of his habit and wiped Father Moreno's face, saying to Father Trujillo: "We must get him to bed."

Father Moreno said, "Look after Pepito, Salvatore. Help him along."

The stricture in his throat prevented Father Trujillo from replying.

Pepito said, "Father Georgio, we are going to take you to your room," and he and Father Trujillo moved to lift him.

"Please—" Father Moreno protested weakly, and suddenly a convulsion seized him. He tried to sit up. "Oh, my brothers!" he whispered imploringly, plainly in great anguish, "pray for me!"

Bending down and speaking through a husky throat, Father Trujillo began to recite rapidly the prayer that commends the soul to God. Father Moreno responded quietly. And when Father Trujillo had concluded the entreaty, the dying man put a hand out to him. "God be praised," he whispered without opening his eyes. "I am at peace." And then, as an afterthought, he said, "I'm sorry about our church, Salvatore." Father Trujillo sobbed, his crucifix against his lips. "Have faith," Father Moreno said weakly. He was having difficulty breathing. "God will help you rebuild it." For a few moments no one spoke, the moans of the injured filling the void. Finally, without opening his eyes, Father Moreno said, "Pepito—"

"Yes, Father?"

"Have faith in God."

"Yes, Father."

"And in thyself."

These were his last words.

CHAPTER TWENTY-SIX

The adz-hewn box containing the remains of Father Moreno was placed on a catafalque before the altar in the chapel and all day mourners came with bouquets of wild-flowers to pay their respects; they brought lupin and owl's clover and moonflowers, mustard, geranium, thistles and bindweed and, to quote Ignacio, "scattered enough pollen to make the dead man sneeze." In filing past the casket each neophyte would kiss the ring on the corpse's left hand, as instructed, and cry out, "Holy Father!" in painful lament. Because they believed that Father Moreno had magical powers, a number of the natives wanted something from his person to ward off evil spirits; and, after his rosary, breviary and sashcord had been pilfered, a guard was posted at the casket. Even so, locks of his thick white hair somehow disappeared, so that by burial time he was all but shorn.

Led by a cross-bearer and six boys carrying lighted candles, the funeral encircled the ruins of the church before proceeding to the gravesite. Initially the Father President, Father Trujillo, Pepito and the visiting missionaries bore the coffin, but soon they were replaced by the soldiers who in turn gave way to neophytes, because everyone wanted to share in the honor.

Father Tapis delivered the eulogy: "One might not expect to find in this remote, sparsely settled land a truly great man," he began, "and many of you may not have realized what a great and saintly man Father Georgio was. Great men often are not recognized by those closest to them. The world is full of people who confuse greatness with fame or riches, whereas neither notoriety nor gold can make a man great. What made Father Georgio great was his heart. He was full of a warm and healing affection which he bestowed upon every living thing. He could not bear to see a goat suffer, no, not even a coyote. The only rule he followed was the rule of kindness. For the happiness and welfare of others he was always eager to contribute, whereas for himself he asked little more than tolerance. Father Georgio labored all

175

his life for the good of mankind and died a poor man in obscurity. Yet if you judge his worth by his strength of character, by his deeds and by his friends, he was a rich man. Yes, there live on this earth many men richer in gold and more famous than Father Georgio, and yet no one lives today who deserves more to be remembered and revered than this disciple of Jesus Christ. He taught the great lesson that, for it to be joyous, life must be lived in an aura of love. Live it any other way and frustration, disappointment and despair will be yours. So, in Father Georgio's memory, I say to you, love your fellowman, be kind and just to him; do all you can with prudence for him, and you, like Father Georgio, will inherit the kingdom of Heaven."

Once the body had been consigned to the earth, Father Trujillo, along with everyone else, knelt to pray; but as he started his address to God, the enormity of the loss burst upon him and he gave way to tears, trembling as if palsied. His sobs came from deep down and were so heartrending that, after the prayer, which he had to conclude, Father Tapis hastened to console him.

"The Lord's ways are unfathomable," the Father President reminded him. "Trust in the Lord." But even as he spoke them he thought that this was a time when words were inadequate. He took Father Trujillo's arm and led him into the olive grove. A meadowlark and a mocking bird were vying to see which could produce the most imaginative phrases and this duet was counterpointed by the hum of foraging bees.

"I can't understand," Father Trujillo sobbed, as they strolled, his face contorted like a child's, "if God is trying to punish me, why does He make others suffer?"

Father Tapis said, "He is reminding us that every thing on this earth is ephemeral, that only love endures. The lesson he is stressing is: though Father Georgio is gone, the love he generated will go on through all of us into eternity."

"He put so much of himself into the church for God's glory," Father Trujillo said, tears streaming down his cheeks, "and now the church is gone."

"But the love he put into it is not gone, Salvatore; it lies even now among the fallen stones. What is important," Father Tapis went on quickly, "is that you built the church. How long it stood is of little matter."

"God must know that, even though we are priests, we have a breaking point."

"Perhaps He is trying to find out what it is."

The anguished priest stopped. "Father," he said imploringly, "would you do something for me? I realize how badly you need missionaries, but would you relieve me? Would you let me go back to the College? Please? I don't have the courage to go on here."

"You cannot find courage by running away, Salvatore."

"I implore you to let me rekindle my faith and my hope. The ship that was to have taken Father Georgio—let me go in his stead."

Father Tapis did not reply at once. He watched a small rabbit come out of a clump of cactus and, pausing wide-eyed, skurry off white-tailed down the orchard. Finally he said, "It is asking much of our brother to leave him here alone."

"I know! I know! I shouldn't go!"

"But you have served here long and well, and if you wish to go I will not hold you."

Father Trujillo took one of the Father President's hands in both his own and kissed it gratefully. "Thank you, Father."

When Father Trujillo sought out Pepito and told him he was returning to Mexico, Pepito said, "If it is what you want, I am happy for you. For me, I am sad."

"You are young and not yet acquainted with the withering power of discouragement," Father Trujillo told him. "You are a Californian. You understand these people. You can lead them."

"I shall do the best I can, of course."

"You are fresh. You have the heart to rebuild the church. And the people will help you. But don't make the mistake I made, Pepe. Don't put your whole heart into it or into anything temporal." Father Trujillo nodded toward the rubble. "Years of sweat and strain."

"The roof was too heavy," Pepito said.

"We thought it would stand forever. Sinner that I am, I looked upon the church as justification for my existence, a monument to myself. God did not take long to show me the error of my ways." And after a pause he said, "Please, I ask you not to say anything of my going. I want to slip unnoticed."

"But you must say good-bye to your children, Father."

"I don't think my departure will make much difference to them."

"Of course it will! They love you, as they loved Father Georgio."

"You are very kind, but I prefer to leave without ceremony."

Inevitably word of Father Trujillo's leaving got around and, coming so soon after Father Moreno's death, it created a furor among the neophytes. A procession of them, all imploring him to stay, followed him to the bay. Women offered their babies as an inducement and men and women kissed his hands and tried to kiss his moving feet to show their veneration. "Don't leave us, Father!—Please, please don't leave us!" they cried, many of them weepingly. "We will work and come to church and say our prayers and eat only fish Fridays!"

Father Trujillo was so moved by this heart-wrenching demonstration that when he came to say good-bye his voice was husky with emotion. He had gotten into the skiff which was to take him to the ship and was standing with arms outstretched. "Farewell, my friends. I leave you my heart. It is in you and it is in the ruins of the church and in the grave of Father Georgio. Remember me kindly and mention me in your prayers, as I shall remember you in mine." He then kissed his crucifix, held it aloft, sat down in the boat. Two soldiers helped the sailor shove the skiff into the water; the sailor jumped in, grasped the oars and rowed hard to get through the first swell. A number of neophytes began chanting the Psalm Father Trujillo had so laboriously taught them: "The Lord is my shepherd, I shall not want. . ." and they sang with such artless sincerity and their words were so full of religiosity that it filled the priest with joy. This poignance was intensified when, still pleading with the priest, some of the young people plunged into the water and swam after him.

"They must mean it, Father," the sailor said, rowing. "There's nothing an Indian hates more than being cold."

And suddenly Father Trujillo realized that he could no more leave San Simeon than he could escape his own destiny. In truth, they were one and the same. These were his people, his family, and here was his home. This realization had an instantaneous and miraculous effect: the hopelessness and despair which had seized him fell away and there surged through him a strong feeling of religious rapture.

The skiff approached the ship. The shaggy-bearded captain was at the gunwale to welcome him aboard. The priest grasped the rope-ladder but made no move to clamber up it. "The Lord has changed my mind," he said, speaking loudly. "I am not going with you."

The captain cupped a hand behind an ear. "What's that you say?"

"I say, the Lord has decided I should not go. I'm staying here."

"You're not going?"

The priest nodded. "I'm not going."

178

The captain was confused. "You're going to stay here?"

"God just told me to stay here."

The skipper shrugged to divest himself of responsibility and spoke to the sailor. "Take him back. And make haste." He saluted the priest. "Good luck."

"Thank you." Father Trujillo made the sign of the cross. "God speed."

From the shore the neophytes saw the skiff with the priest still in it turn about and head for shore. They watched silently, uncertainly, hopefully. Why was he coming back? Had he forgotten something?

Even before he stepped onto the sand, Father Trujillo shouted to those on shore: "I'm going to stay! God would not let me go!" and there went up such a vociferous expression of joy and jubilaton that it drowned out the sound of the spewing waves.

Pepito embraced his brother priest and together they set out for the Mission, followed by the excited Californians. As they strode along Father Trujillo spoke enthusiastically of rebuilding the church as a memorial to Father Moreno and he rattled on happily about training Inez's son Lucas to be an altar boy. "He is a bright lad," he said. "Unlike his father, I think he will serve God well."

"Perhaps," Pepito said, "with your guidance he will become a priest." And looking up at the darkening sky, he added, "You know, Father, I think the Lord is about to bless us with rain."

*　*　*